CW00616969

000000593097

DANGER VALLEY

DANGER VALLEY

DANGER VALLEY

Richard Poole

GUNSMOKE

First published in the US by Doubleday

This hardback edition 2012
by AudioGO Ltd
by arrangement with
Golden West Literary Agency

ISBN 978 1 471 32048 4

British Library Cataloguing in Publication Data available.

Printed and bound in Great Britain by
MPG Books Group Limited

DANGER VALLEY

DANGER VALLEY

I

When they topped the low ridge on their return to the ranch house, Greg Corwin reined in and Hobe Terrall, with an over-the-shoulder look of surprise, pulled his horse half around, bleak eyes narrowing in something like fright and suspicion.

"Something wrong?"

The younger man shook his head. He sat tall and slender in the saddle, gaze slowly ranging east to west along the high sharp line of mountains marking the northern boundary of Sioux Valley. Rich graze broken by timbered areas made windbreaks against the snows and blizzards of winter, low hills broke the valley into distinct areas. Greg's chest lifted with his full breath, softly expelled and his tawny eyes grew soft.

Terrall's husky voice broke the silence. "This is all Tumbling T range north to the Dark Hills. Can't see 'em. Hidden by that timber coming down from the northeast. County seat's five miles beyond."

Greg, still drinking in the country ahead and below, asked, "How about the neighbors?"

The old rancher indicated directions. "Bar Y, the biggest, bounds us north and east, the town's right on its boundary. Rest of the spreads about the size of Tumbling T; Anchor over there—Rocking Chair up that way. South and west, four smaller outfits. All of 'em doing good but, of course, Bar Y ships the most cattle out of Sioux Valley."

"Where's shipping point?"

"Thirty miles north of the valley. But it's no drive at all. Good graze and clear road all the way, even through the mountains. I never had no trouble—and no one else."

Greg's sudden smile softened angular jaw and chin, lifted to his eyes in a sparkling glow. "Let's get back to the house."

He spurred his horse to a trot and Terrall caught up with him a few yards farther on. The old man shrewdly appraised the young stranger, approving of the broad shoulders, muscular back and arms, remembering long ago when his own had been as powerful. As Corwin half turned to look off to the west, Terrall noted the smooth way in which his torso moved and the jut of jaw and chin suggesting courage—or stubbornness. Terrall's dry lips faintly twisted. Corwin would need both if he stayed in Sioux Valley.

The old man's wrinkled face grew bland when Corwin threw another question. Now, the two riders crossed a grass rich swale and threaded between low hills. The vista ahead opened as they broke free of the hills and again Greg Corwin reined in.

Terrall, curbing impatience, stopped just beside him. Below, and across the wide swale, stood the buildings of Tumbling T. Corwin studied them, trying to see them coldly through a mounting inner excitement. The buildings looked solid and sturdy, from rambling ranch house and bunkhouse under the trees to the few corrals, the barn and work-buildings.

Terrall couldn't help asking, "Like the looks of it?"

"Range and buildings, yes. But the beef tally—"

2

"You're a cattleman. When's tally ever exactly right until round-up or a head count? I won't hold to the book figure. I try to be fair."

Corwin chuckled like an eager boy as he looked slowly over the valley in another slow, circling sweep. His deep voice held a new vibrancy. "Let's get to the house and talk."

Terrall moved ahead. Unseen by Corwin, his seamed face showed relief, and he swiped a gnarled hand across his mouth, letting uncertainty and tension ease out in a long, soft sigh. They trotted into the ranch yard, reined in before the house. An old cowboy sat in the late afternoon sun before the bunkhouse door, watching Terrall and the stranger ground-tie their horses and move to the house.

Terrall pushed open the heavy door and stepped into the big main room ahead of Corwin. He turned as Corwin closed the door behind him and swept off his hat, revealing black hair, sweat damp where the hatband had pressed. Terrall said sharply, "You're ready to talk business?"

"I'm ready to make the deal, Terrall—pending one question."

"First, let me throw one. You're a puncher—worked for wages and it ain't likely a hired rider has the kind of money I want for Tumbling T. I ain't going to fool around with mortgages and notes and such. All of it cold cash. Are we wasting one another's time?"

The young man dropped his hat on a chair, pulled his faded, checked shirt out of his trousers, revealing a money belt around his slender waist. He unbuckled it, opened one of the leather pouches and produced banknotes. Terrall's eyes bugged slightly and he said dryly, "Drinks are on me. Come on."

He led the way down a short corridor to a small room that served as ranch office. He waved Corwin to one of the two chairs and Greg sat down. The window faced him and

3

he could look directly at the bunkhouse many yards away, see a corner of the stable and the corrals beyond.

Terrall pulled a whiskey bottle and glasses from the bottom drawer of the scarred rolltop desk, poured, handed a glass to Greg. "Here's to a dicker."

They drank and Terrall settled deep in a cushioned chair before the desk. "I've showed you my range and beef. You've seen the house and the buildings. You're getting a steal."

"Why? What haven't you showed me or told me?"

"I ain't hid nothing, Corwin. Why? Because I've worked myself half crippled, first for forty and found and then building up this spread. I could stay until I die, but the ranch'd go to the Territory, I reckon. No heirs. Doc tells me to get out of Wyoming—head to the desert. So I'm willing for hard cash to cut price and take care of myself down around Tucson somewhere. That satisfy you?"

Greg saw, through the window, the rolling spread of rich graze beyond the buildings, a far line of timber. His eyes glowed. "Sounds better than fair. How about crew?"

"Your problem. They're free to sign on with you or ride off. If they stay, you got a good bunch. If they leave, others can be hired in Redman."

"I'll see how much payroll I can meet."

"Your problem again. Now—you buying Tumbling T?"

"Yes."

Terrall nodded, choking back an audible sigh of relief. He covered it by swinging to the desk and taking paper and pen. "First, I'll do a bill of sale and receipt. Then deed and order to change title. Got the abstract right here."

He turned to a small iron safe, whirled the knobs and opened the door. He took out a thick bundle of papers. "Represents homestead grants and transfers, some graze I bought twenty years ago. Altogether, it's the range you saw."

As Terrall busied himself writing, the younger man

4

walked to the window, looked out on the yard. His chest rose on a deep breath, fell—and at that moment he took possession. He noticed the old man and two stubble-beard punchers near the door of the bunkhouse.

Terrall dropped his pen. "There it is. Count out the money and sign this acknowledgment."

Greg dropped the bills on the desk. He counted the gold-backs, Terrall with him, shoved the thick neat pile to the old man's hand. Terrall touched the money, had a sudden doubt. "This *is* yours, Corwin? I mean . . ."

"It's mine. Not stolen." Corwin laughed, a clear, clean sound. "I won it, Terrall. Two days and three nights at a saloon table in Colorado."

"Won it! No working puncher has gambling stakes big enough to sit in a game—"

"Started low, friend. Me'n a big rancher—owns two spreads down there and another in Texas—got stuck in a crossroads town in a blizzard. We started for pennies. I kept winning. It rowelled his pride for he figured *no one* had *his* poker savvy. I tried to break off at first but then the excitement became something between him and me—more'n cards, luck and savvy. When the blizzard and the game ended, I had his ready cash and drafts on his bank."

"I'm damned!"

"Know exactly how you feel. Here I had goldbacks more'n I ever dreamed of—me! Working for beans and a blanket! Always hoped someday I could buy a spread with a few head, maybe. But this! I told my boss to get himself another cowpoke and I headed here."

"Why?"

Greg leaned back. "Sioux Valley—right out there through the window! Heard about it a dozen times and dreamed of it like you would of heaven or a red headed girl when you're winter-bogged in a line shack. So, I come looking."

5

"To Redman?" Terrall asked sharply and his fingers covered the money.

"No, came up through the South Pass. Met a rider from some spread down there—don't know which one—and when I asked about buying range, he told me Tumbling T might consider a reasonable offer. I come here."

Terrall's bony fingers relaxed. He pushed the bill of sale and abstract to Greg as he picked up the yellowbacks. "Better ride to Redman and register deed and sale with the County Recorder along with the brand transfer. Ain't yours by record until that's done. Actually, I reckon as of this minute I'm a visitor at *your* ranch."

"And welcome! I'll head out for Redman come morning. Can you put me up?"

"I told you, it's *your* house! Can you put me up? I'll head out soon myself. Maybe you want to meet the crew."

"Later, when I get back from Redman. Right now—"

"Another drink and chow." Terrall stood up. "Mind my cooking? Crew takes care of itself in the bunkhouse."

"Not if it's as good as your whiskey."

After supper, during which Terrall gave Greg more detailed information about the ranch operations, the valley, his neighbors and the size of their spreads, the two had another drink and then Terrall took Greg to a bedroom in one wing of the house.

Greg slowly undressed, pausing often to look about the room, assuring himself everything was *his*. He finally blew out the lamp and walked to the window. Now he could see and sense the dark spread of the land out there, his range. His eyes caressed the night-darkened shapes of the outbuildings and lifted to the clear Wyoming stars. He took a deep, ecstatic breath and reluctantly groped his way to the bed.

He was up at dawn and helped Terrall fix breakfast, listening to more pointers about the ranch and valley as the old man remembered them. Greg wolfed down the food and hurried out to the corral, Terrall trailing him. Greg swung into the saddle and rode out of the corral and yard. He followed the ranch road until it joined with a wider, dirt road leading north to Redman.

He studied the crude sign reading, "Tumbling T—Hobe Terrall." That would soon be changed, he thought, and touched the thick bundle of papers in his pocket. He spoke to the bay and set himself for the ride to the distant town.

He rode through strange country, judging it—grass, low, rolling hills, timber, arms of which reached out across the road that cut through it, trees forming a pleasant arch overhead. Just beyond, he came on a stone cairn built beside the road. One rock was flat and a black Bar Y had been painted on its surface.

His neighbors, Greg thought as he rode by. He'd make a call as soon as all the legal registering and filing was done. With the thought came the stunning realization that he was now rancher himself—landowner, businessman, meeting with his own kind in Redman. There'd be a saloon, he knew, where ordinary punchers would not go—the kind he had never been in before. It made him feel a little nervous.

"You still think like wages, Corwin," he growled aloud at himself.

Greg crossed another rich swale and, in the distance, saw grazing beef, probably Bar Y stock. The road led to another line of hills, higher and more jagged. Just before he entered a canyon, a smaller road led off east for a distance and then curved to plunge into a distant defile. A solid, firm sign pointed a wooden finger along the road and announced "Bar Y." The hills loomed on either side, sometimes bare clay cuts, again falling back in heavily wooded slopes. The road curved to wind around the hill spurs, giving the feel of dark and rugged country.

A flat, sharp crack of sound came suddenly. A second

7

later, echoes of it followed. Greg pulled up, head lifting, ears keened. He knew the sound of a rifle shot. Hunters? Instantly three or four distant reports denied the question and they were followed by a softer, deeper note—that of a Colt in answer.

Gunfight . . . up ahead.

Greg's hand automatically dropped to the holstered gun at his side. He heard no repetition of the sound for long minutes, wondered if the disturbance ahead was over, debated whether he should ride into it.

Then the flat explosions broke the silence and once more the Colt replied with a single shot. Greg judged several riflemen ahead and just one target. He worked his lips, uncertain. No one but Terrall knew him in Sioux Valley and riding up on whatever happened ahead could be exactly the wrong thing to do.

The rifles sounded again, receiving the reply of the single shot. Many against one. Greg rubbed his hand along the holstered Colt, glanced down at his rifle in the boot, then gently touched spurs. The bay moved slowly forward, Greg searching the wooded slopes to either side as well as the twisting road ahead.

He came to a sharp turn and suddenly the fusillade broke out again, this time so close it sounded like thunder. Greg swung out of saddle, ground-tied the bay and eased forward along the edge of the road around the turn.

Ahead, the road ran straight across a narrow swale bounded by high wooded slopes to either side. Greg saw the overturned buggy in the road, the horse lying in the tangled harness. Rifle shots to his left caught his attention. He could not see the marksman and, further along the same slope, two more rifles fired.

His eyes swung to the buggy just as a figure showed head and shoulders and a Colt boomed and belched an ineffectual lance of flame toward the hidden ambushers. Greg's eyes

8

flew wide as his brain registered a slender, curving body briefly outlined against the sun, a cascade of dark hair falling over the shoulders. Then the figure dropped from sight and he saw splinters fly from the buggy as rifles again sought their mark.

A woman!

His wide lips set as his hand slashed to his holstered gun. He jerked it away, wheeled about and ran back to his horse. He swept up reins, led it into the shadows of the trees and snatched the rifle from the boot. He jacked a bullet into the chamber and darted up the slope, disappearing into the trees in a direction that would bring him above and behind the ambushers.

Maybe not his fight but . . . a woman . . . gunned down!

A branch whipped at his face but with tawny eyes, suddenly like those of a predatory cat, he moved with Indian grace and deadliness along the slope.

9

II

A burst of rifle fire along the ridge made him lunge ahead, disregarding the whip of branches and the noise he made. Then he checked his rush as, from below, the single Colt boomed a hopeless return challenge.

Greg placed the position of the riflemen along the ridge among the bushes and trees, still hidden from his sight. He angled sharply up the ridge, moving quietly but swiftly. He stopped short when he caught a movement ahead and below. He had a glimpse of the overturned buggy on the dirt road, then his eyes fastened on a slight movement of bushes just ahead.

Greg lined his rifle on an uncertain form half seen through the screen of leaves. His finger tightened on the trigger and then caution checked him. He had no idea who the girl or her attackers were and he preferred to drive off rather than to kill or wound. He lifted the rifle sights and squeezed off the shot.

He heard a startled yell. The bushes threshed. A man appeared and Greg's second shot whipped so close that the man jerked away. Greg saw a pinched, dark face as the ambusher plunged into the bushes and disappeared. Greg sent a bullet winging after him, high enough to miss but keep the man running. From below, the Colt blasted again.

Greg heard yells farther along. He raced after the threshing sounds of flight. He glimpsed the man, saw another pop out of bushes. Greg stopped short, fired, jacked shell into the chamber and fired a second time, both slugs whipping close to the startled men. They raced up the slope. Beyond them, another shouted a warning and Greg saw an uncertain shadow move among the trees and bushes, the fleeing third ambusher.

He fired high, urging on the flight. He stood, ears keened up the slope. He heard nothing for a moment and then came a muffled beat of hoofs, fading into complete silence. Then the Colt from below boomed, a sheer waste of powder and lead.

Greg turned downslope, now making no attempt at concealment as he threshed through the line of bushes the ambushers had used. The Colt boomed and Greg heard the whip-snap of the heavy slug by his head. A second bullet whipped to his left, a wider miss but still too close. He yelled, "Hey! Down there! Stop shooting!"

His answer came, a bullet that whipped the air beside his shoulder. He dropped flat. "Hey! I'm a friend! I drove those jaspers off!"

Greg came to a crouch. "Can I come out?"

Silence, then a feminine voice with a dangerous edge. "Come out slow and hands up."

Greg's lips flattened angrily but he realized what the woman must be thinking. He slowly rose, pushed through a final screen of leaves and bushes and emerged, hands held at shoulder level.

Just below him, the buggy lay on its side, the dead horse in the shafts. He slowly moved down the slope. He had taken but a few steps when a clipped voice ordered, "Stop

11

right there. I want a look at you. If your friends up in the bushes try anything, you'll get a bullet."

"They're not my friends. Why do you think they ran off?"

"A good question. Just don't move."

Very slowly a crown of dark hair and then a face appeared around the edge of the wrecked vehicle. Greg saw long, planed cheeks, vivid red lips, now hardly more than an angry slash above a pointed, delicate chin. Dark eyes blazed as she stepped clear and the Colt she held lined directly on him.

She wore a plain gray dress, edged with white at collar and sleeves that ended just above the elbows. The dress was rumpled, dirt stained. She was young, curvesome, yet slender. As she moved, the swing and fall of her long dress suggested shapely legs.

A slight lift of the Colt in a hand seemingly too small to hold it brought his eyes to her face. A lock of dark hair fell down over one eye and, with an impatient jerk of head and sweep of free hand, she pushed it back.

Greg saw little flames of anger in her dark eyes. She ventured a sweeping glance beyond him up the slope. A second later she coldly studied him again.

"Satisfied, ma'am?"

"Not quite. Who are you?"

"Name's Greg Corwin. I first saw this valley just three days ago."

"One of Yates' hired gunslingers?"

Greg irritably started to lower his hands but the girl's Colt muzzle lifted suggestively. He checked the movement a second and then, tawny eyes locking with hers, slowly lowered his hands to his sides. The gun muzzle levelled and he saw the swift set of her lips, the tension of her body.

Greg said accusingly, "You're alive because I took a hand, but seems like you don't appreciate it."

The gun wavered slightly. "You didn't answer my question. Did Yates hire you?"

"I brought myself into the Valley, ma'am. Nobody hired me for anything."

"What are you doing here?"

"Looking around—on my own business." He indicated the wrecked buggy and the dead horse. "What were you doing that someone wants to kill you?"

A flush rose in her cheeks and then she slowly lowered the Colt. She wiped the back of her hand across cheek and mouth and Greg could see she stood at the edge of tears. But she held them back. He sensed that her beauty concealed tight self-control.

She wheeled about to the buggy, examining its bullet scars. She looked down at the dead horse and her lips trembled, then tightened. She turned to face him.

"I apologize. I didn't know you helped—too many bullets flying around to tell one from another." She studied him again. "Where are you from, Greg Corwin?"

"Colorado. Came up this way to see what I could find."

"You found a range war. That's why they . . ." She gestured toward the slope. As though that explained everything, she abruptly said, "I'm Amanda Zane. I run Rocking Chair while my father recovers from another bushwhack bullet."

Greg made a soundless whistle. "I heard Sioux Valley was always a place a man could dream about for ranching."

"Nightmares now. You'd be smart to ride out, Mr. Corwin. Unless . . ." She looked at him with new appraisal. "Where's your horse?"

"Back there. And you made me leave my rifle up the slope."

"Get them."

She turned away with the flat order. Greg watched her skirt the buggy and disappear behind it. He heard sounds

13

that told him she gathered up scattered contents. He balanced a second and then turned away. He recovered his rifle, then moved down the road to his horse and led it back to the buggy. The girl had dragged flour sack, canned goods and supplies into a small pile and stood waiting for him. Wind blew the dress against her body, streamed dark hair back over her shoulders. She stood straight and proud, belying her slenderness and femininity.

When Greg came up, she said, "Can I owe you another favor? I need to get home."

"Glad to ride you there, ma'am. But what about that?"

She dismissed the pile of supplies with a shrug. "Yates hires killers but he doesn't steal. I'll send a rider and buckboard for it. Anyone passing will know the buggy, and poor Darby has the Rocking Chair brand on his flank. They'll know what Yates has done. He's made his first bad mistake."

Greg accepted the statement. She placed a slender slipper in the stirrup and with an easy grace swung herself up and into the saddle. He mounted behind her, gingerly placed his hands on the cantle but she said impatiently, "I won't break, Mr. Corwin, and I intend to ride fast. This is no time to be bashful."

She kicked the bay's ribs and it lunged forward. He eased his arm about her waist. It was narrow and supple and her blowing hair whipped back against his face. She held to the fast pace until the pass through the hills opened onto another swale. Then she cut off the road, heading south and west. Far enough to escape detection from the road, she slowed the bay to an easy walk to Greg's relief. He removed his arm and held to the cantle again.

She spoke over her shoulder. "You acted fast back there, Mr. Corwin. They could have turned on you."

"Surprise, ma'am, that's all. Maybe you'll tell me what it's all about?"

14

"Barton Yates wants Rocking Chair and all the rest of Sioux Valley."

"At gun point? Seems there'd be an easier way to get it."

"Why buy out when you can run out? That's what Bar Y is doing. They've put my father out of action, leaving me to run the spread. If I was killed by those gunhawks—"

"If they intended to kill," Greg cut in, "they could have circled you easy and you'd have no place to hide. No, more like scaring you off."

She rode, body swaying to the movement of the horse. She answered thoughtfully, "You might be right. But, still, it's range war and in the open now. I didn't figure Rocking Chair was next."

Greg thought of Hobe Terrall and the surprisingly cheap price of Tumbling T. "Who was to be next?"

Her shoulders lifted, fell and Greg brushed a lock of her hair from his face. "Tumbling T, if I had to guess. It'd be logical but maybe Yates figured that would be the very reason I'd be careless. And I was!"

Greg's jaw set. "How long has this been going on?"

"Since Yates was hired to ramrod Bar Y. But he wouldn't move without Vale Edwards giving the order. Vale's the owner." She pointed east and south. "Two small spreads down there have been swallowed up—one sold out and the other got killed. No heirs, so Bar Y bought it through the courts. Now Tumbling T just south of us. I'm further west and beyond me is Anchor. Unless we get together and fight, it will all be Bar Y before long."

"What about Tumbling T?"

"Hobe Terrall!" she flung back over her shoulder in contempt. "If Yates so much as growls in his direction, Terrall will run. I'd bet on it. But there's no sign Bar Y has made any move in that direction."

Greg held to the cantle and glared beyond the girl's shoulder at the range country to the south. His range! the deed,

15

sale and abstract in his saddlebag. He had been tricked—not lied to but certainly not told any part of the situation.

He began to have second thoughts. He answered the girl's questions about himself with brief words. They came to a road and Amanda Zane turned the horse into it. Greg tried to consider the situation with detachment. He wondered if he should take the word of this girl without question. Something warned him not to make decision or take sides until he knew more about Sioux Valley. After all, he had talked only to Hobe Terrall and now to Amanda Zane—who said convincingly that Terrall feared Bar Y.

But—what about Bar Y? Did Amanda Zane jump to unwarranted conclusions stemming from some fancied slight or attack in the past? The three ambushers were certainly not figments of the imagination but what was the proof they worked for Bar Y and Barton Yates, whoever he was? The attack could stem from some other quarrel or be an attempt by three lawless drifters to rob a lone woman driving across the range.

The girl suddenly checked the intense working of his brain. "There's my road. We're a mile up in those hills. What are your plans, Mr. Corwin?"

"I don't know."

"Consider a job? I'm short a hand and Rocking Chair will need a good rifle like yours before long. I pay top wages."

They approached the hills and the wide curve of the road between them. "I don't think so, ma'am."

She twisted about to search his face. He became aware of deep pools of brown eyes, of the delicate curve of cheekbone, and her lips, uncomfortably close, moved to ask, "Why not? A good job and a clean ranch. Oh, you think I want to buy your gun?"

"Well . . . maybe that's one thing—"

"I'm forced to, Mr. Corwin. You saw what happened today. But that will pass—soon, I hope. Then it'll be just a clean, good job of riding for Rocking Chair and no more."

Greg saw the ranch ahead; a small house, bunkhouse and buildings, not quite as big as Tumbling T. They rode through the open gate and approached the house. A man appeared in the barn door and strode out to meet them. She drew rein and Greg jumped down, as the puncher strode up, and turned to help Amanda dismount. But she had already swung out of the saddle and dropped to her feet, eagerly facing him. "About that job—"

"No, ma'am. You put it nice but still you're buying a gun."

"I told you why and—"

He gathered up the reins. "I've got business of my own, ma'am—important business. Glad to have been of help."

He stepped into the saddle. The approaching puncher stopped short, questioning eyes flicking from Amanda to Greg, who touched his hat brim to her, reined about and spurred the bay into a fast trot.

He didn't look back but he felt the girl's angry eyes following after him, scorching into the middle of his back.

17

III

———◆———

At the junction of the Rocking Chair and the main road, Greg drew rein and looked about, placing the lay of the Valley in his mind. With an angry grunt, he set the bay off the road on a beeline to a showdown with Hobe Terrall.

At long last, Greg broke through one of the inevitable groves of trees and saw Tumbling T buildings ahead. He pulled in, face grim as he looked at the distant ranch yard. Anger mounted again and he knew he must control it before he faced Terrall.

Finally, he rode slowly down the slope. He felt a tight, controlled calm. Greg expected to see Terrall or one of his crew appear but there was no hail. He had the feeling that the buildings stood empty and abandoned. He frowned, not liking the brooding air that hovered over the ranch. Now he could see the corral. The hoof-pocked area was as empty of life as the rest of the ranch. Then he heard a muffled stomp from within the stable adjoining the corral and Greg eased down in the saddle. That brown haired Amanda Zane had spooked him! he thought with a wry grin.

The momentary relief evaporated as he circled the corral

18

to come up to the house from the rear. Again he felt the sense of empty and abandoned home. Windows and doors were closed. His head swivelled to the bunkhouse to his left, seemingly just as empty though the door was open.

A man appeared within the doorway, the old puncher Greg had seen once before. The man stood a moment and then stepped out as Greg swung the bay around. He asked, "Where's Terrall?"

"Gone." Leathery jaws worked a moment and then the dry voice added, "Yonderly—somewhere—maybe headed for Tucson. Place ain't his no more. It's yours."

"But—"

Greg's lips snapped shut and he dismounted and scowled about at the silent buildings. "Where's the crew?"

"I'm it. Rest took their pay and rode out with Hobe. Just you and me—and that depends on whether you want me to stay on."

Greg eyed the man a moment. "You'll do."

"Decide that later, seeing I'm a mite stove up. My name's Weber . . . Cal, short for California where I always aimed to go but never made it. . . . Plenty of stable space and the house is all yours, like bunkhouse is all mine. Welcome to your new home."

"Thanks. Maybe you and me had better talk about it—and this whole valley. Hang around."

He led the horse to the stable. The interior held the day's waning heat and the good clean smell of hay and horse. A line of empty stalls faced Greg to the right and all but one on the left were empty. A gray horse pushed out a curious head and whinnied a greeting to the bay.

When Greg emerged, Cal Weber leaned against a corner of the bunkhouse but straightened as Greg came striding up. He fished a ring of keys from his pocket. "Hobe said give you these."

Greg took them and led the way to the house. The rear

19

door was unlocked and he stepped into the spacious kitchen. The house boomed with the sound of his and Weber's steps. Greg led the way to the office, stepped in and looked about.

Cal suggested, "Hobe left his whiskey in the desk drawer and there's more in the kitchen cupboard. He said you might need it."

"What do you think?"

"Hobe always knew what he was doing."

"I believe you."

Greg pulled open the lower desk drawer and saw the bottle and half a dozen shot glasses. He filled two, passed one to Cal Weber. Greg lifted his in a mock salute and downed it in a gulp. Cal drank more slowly, sitting in a chair Greg indicated.

Greg refilled the glasses but only moved his about in his fingers. "On the way to Redman, I ran into a bushwhack—three men trying for a woman, Amanda Zane."

"Kill a woman! They'd go that far!"

"I figure trying to drive her off. That's neither here nor there. I bought a range war, not a ranch, didn't I?"

"You bought both."

"Terrall should've told me, damn him!"

Cal sipped at his drink. "You should've rode around and asked people before you bought, for that matter."

Greg glared a second then eased down in his chair with a wry smile. "I'll ask you. Thinking of the Zane woman, I'd say it's bad."

"Could be a little worse—like beef killing, fence cutting, ranch burning and night riding."

"Will it be?"

"Depends—on what Bar Y and Amanda Zane do."

"She wants to hire my guns."

"Figures. She's trying to line up the whole valley against Bar Y. Since her Paw took a bullet, she's hell bent to get Barton Yates. Don't blame her."

20

"Her father? Open fight or ambush?"

"Nothing open here yet."

Greg settled more firmly in his chair. "Start from the beginning."

"That'd be when Barton Yates was hired to ramrod Bar Y."

"Who owns it?"

"Vale Edwards. In the old days, him and Hobe Terrall helped drive the Sioux out of this part of the country. Vale's the older, a lot older. Wife's dead. Has a daughter. Good looking redhead but so damn' proud she's too good for any rancher or puncher in these parts. Ain't married."

"Her problem. Mine's Barton Yates, the way I see it."

"Not so sure. What foreman works without the bosses orders?"

"But what about him?"

The old man looked out the window as he took a long moment to round up the facts. "Like Hobe, Vale Edwards is old and stiff in the joints. Had a foreman almost as old as him but Edwards let him run Bar Y—until the foreman couldn't take these winters no more and he had to quit. Barton Yates was hired."

"Where's he from?"

"Somewhere yonderly. Young man—and big. He didn't drift in, understand. Vale had word of him from somewhere. Yates had the job before he rode into Sioux Valley. Right away, all of us could tell he took hold. Bar Y had started to get ragged but Yates stopped that. He hired a whole new crew. Then he had Edwards buy a couple of baling-wire outfits to the east and one to the north. That was the first sign of what Bar Y had in mind—but we didn't read it right."

"And the second sign?"

"Bar L, to the north. Joe Lehman, the owner, was found shot. Some said he run into rustlers from over the Sioux Range. Lehman lived alone and first thing we knew, Bar Y had Bar L. So talk started. Next, a rancher to the north found his road cut off over Bar Y range. He couldn't bring supplies in, cattle out or even ride to town—himself and his two punchers. Starved out and sold out, the way we read it."

"Barton Yates?"

"Up in front, anyhow. But—behind him?" Cal placed his empty glass on the edge of the desk. "Rocking Chair next. Yates offered a price to Harry Zane and was turned down flat. Things began to happen. Barn caught fire—no one knows how. Beef died—poisoned tank but no one knows who did it. Then Harry got shot—crippled him bad. Harry says he saw Yates and a Bar Y brand on the horse. But Yates denied it— proved he was twenty miles away."

"How'd he prove it?"

"Sheriff didn't say exactly. But—that ended it."

He let Greg study that for a moment and then continued. "Amanda took charge and, let me tell you, she gets things done. She'll fight man or woman that gets in her way. She's been riding over the whole Valley to get the small ranchers to band against Bar Y."

"For what? Destroy it? Shoot-out of some kind?"

"More like banding together for protection. If Bar Y tries for one, it tries for them all. She was here a dozen times but Hobe figured he'd only make it worse for himself if he tied in with her."

"Because Bar Y—?"

"Yates offered to buy Tumbling T. No threats. Just rode in, friendly, to make a business proposition. He's like that. Came back three more times—last, a week ago and he wasn't near so friendly."

"And then—?"

"You rode in. What'd you pay?"

Greg told him. "It was a damn' reasonable price for a place like this, as I saw it."

"And twice more'n Bar Y offered."

22

Greg pushed up from the chair and strode to the window. He looked out on the ranch yard and nearby bunkhouse. My ranch, he thought with an angry grimace. But for how long? He had another thought, turned sharply. "Cal, why do you stay when all the rest rode off?"

"Like I said, too old to run." The leathery face worked and the faded eyes looked embarrassed. "And maybe something that don't make sense. First time in all the years I've known him, Hobe didn't show clear sign all the way. Not that he *had* to tell you about Bar Y, understand, but that he should."

"And you want to pay his debt?"

"No one can do that for any man. But, say, I don't want to leave you in a trap. It's for my feeling toward myself, not for Hobe. Not that a stove-up jasper like me could do much good but—"

"You'll do."

Cal smiled his thanks, no more. It was enough. The two men remained silent a moment and then Cal slowly stood up. "Well, you know how the sign reads but it ain't my part to tell you what to do about it. I'd best leave you to plan your own trail."

"Choice of two, looks like. Throw in with Amanda Zane and her friends to fight Bar Y. Or sell out to Bar Y unless I want to go under like the others have."

"That's about it—fight or run. Like I said, your decision."

23

IV

Greg sat alone before the desk, deep into the problem that had been so unexpectedly presented. He wheeled about in the chair so that he could look out into the clear blue sky. He hardly heard the closing of the kitchen door as Cal left the house.

For a time, Greg could not bring his mind down to the problem itself because he had to battle the knowledge that he had been cheated—by Hobe Terrall and, in some way he couldn't quite shape, by life itself. His chance to make a dream come true had been snatched away just as he thought he had that dream in his hands.

Gradually, Greg's basic good sense cut through his churning emotions and he could begin to see the elements of the trap into which he had fallen. He had a mental picture of the road and the overturned buggy, the hidden riflemen searching out Amanda Zane. That represented one element and, Greg knew, rifles could as easily be turned on him as on the girl.

Old Cal Weber had suggested the second element—Bar Y had made an offer for this ranch and, presumably, Greg could also accept it. But, if Cal had been right, he would lose half the money with which he had come into Sioux Valley. Half his money, he repeated to himself, but he could lose all of it if he refused.

His fingers absently beat a broken rhythm on the chair arm as he looked unseeingly toward the far lift of the mountains. To take the half and run would leave him without enough to buy a decent ranch—and run it—anywhere, even beyond Sioux Valley.

He had come here following a long-time dream. Should he leave? He looked about at the desk, the office, the small safe in the corner with its key lock. He fished out the keys Cal had given him and soon had the safe open, the ranch books spread out on the desk.

The day darkened toward evening but Greg hardly noticed as he worked through the figures of sales, expenses, tallies. He was startled when Cal spoke from the doorway. "Getting on towards supper. Shall I fix chow in the kitchen?"

Shadows were dark in the corners of the office and Greg strained to see the ledger figures. He pushed them back and arose. "I'll help you. Why don't you move into the house? No point in us yelling back and forth from one building to another."

Cal's eyes lighted and he turned away with a nod. By the time supper had been cooked and they ate at the table near the kitchen window, the lamp was lit and, outside, star-filled night weighed down on the valley. They sat over coffee and rolled cigarettes.

Greg said, "From what I see in the books, Terrall made money."

"Not as much as in the old days, but beef prices were high then. Yep, he did all right from what I could see."

"How many hands kept it going?"

"Four, counting Hobe and me. But until fall round-up,

25

two of us could keep it going. Might have us humping considerable, but it could be done."

Greg studied the old puncher, judging his strength and stamina. "And at round-up?"

"Full crew and maybe four more. Lots of range and breaks to cover and a heap of beef. Hobe's tally is honest."

"Between now and fall—you won't mind the extra work?"

"Might take some linament and salve now and then but—helll—what else is there to do? No, I'd string along. Is that what you're figuring on doing?"

"That depends on Bar Y—Vale Edwards, if I remember his name."

"Then both of us had better start riding chuckline yonderly. Vale's out to get the whole valley."

"I've heard you say it—and Amanda Zane. I haven't heard him say it."

That night and the next morning he refused to elaborate, though Cal couldn't suppress surprised questions. Cal watched after Greg as he rode away from the ranch. Greg came to the smaller but well kept road marked with the Bar Y sign and looked ahead to where it disappeared into a cleft of the hills. He looked back toward his own range and then straightened, jaw out-thrust and hand tight on the reins.

He threaded the hills, following the road. He constantly scanned the turns ahead, the slopes, sometimes clear and grassy, again pressing close with tree, rocks, or both. His hand never moved far from the Colt in his holster.

There was no alarm, no sound, and Greg hoped there would be no trouble—at least until he reached the Bar Y ranch house itself. Still, he glanced sharply down side canyons and swales, many of them choked with brush and trees.

He made a turn and, far ahead, saw that the road plunged out into one of the many secondary valleys making up the whole Sioux Valley complex. He knew his goal would soon be in sight, for Cal had described the landmarks. His chest rose in a deep breath and he urged the bay forward, increasing its pace. He held his gaze to the distant canyon opening, anticipating his first sight of the Bar Y buildings. He passed a side canyon with a careless glance at the covering of saplings.

He made a spasmodic, upright jerk as a gun blasted and a bullet whistled high over his head. His hand dropped to his Colt but a voice called, "Freeze!"

His hand jerked away as his eyes widened with added surprise. A woman's voice—Amanda Zane again! He started to twist about but the voice repeated, "Freeze! I mean it. Let me see your hands above your hat brim."

"Look, yesterday—"

The roar of the gun cut him short, the bullet closer this time. His lips flattened in irritation but he slowly lifted his hands. When the Zane girl saw who it was, he'd tell her to look first and then . . .

She came up from behind him. It was not Amanda Zane. This one had coppery red hair, swirling down and up under a black, flat-crowned hat caught by a leather thong under a small but determined chin. He became aware of clear blue eyes regarding him with harsh suspicion and, also, he thought, with an uncertainty she tried to hide.

But the gun in her small fist was very certain and dead-centered on his chest. Above it, he saw a white blouse, loose fitting over a full, curvesome torso. She wore a puncher's blue denim levis, held by a wide belt around a slender waist. She sat her saddle like a veteran and held the Colt as though she knew only too well how to use it.

Her lips, full, soft and aglow with natural color, shaped a harsh question. "Where are you going?"

"Bar Y."

"You don't belong here, mister. Are you another trouble hunter?"

"Now what does that mean?"

"A gun-drifter our neighbors"—she said the word with acid scorn—"hire to throw a slug now and then at our riders."

"No one hires me for guns or riding. I'm my own boss."

"Chucklining? We have a full crew and you're wasting your time."

"Your Colt makes me believe it, ma'am. But I'm not looking for work. I want to see Vale Edwards."

"I'm Diana Edwards, his daughter. You can talk to me."

He studied her and a faint blush touched her neck under his direct eyes. Her lips subtly softened but then firmed against a feminine pleasure at his regard, something instinctive she could not fully hide.

"Begging pardon, ma'am. But I'll save what I say for Mr. Edwards himself."

Her eyes sparked and then became uncertain. He wiggled his fingers above his hat brim. "Kind of tiring, ma'am. And I intend a palaver, not war."

Her body stiffened and the black gun muzzle held steadily on his chest. She spoke with firmness. "Lower one hand . . . slow. Unbuckle your gunbelt. Easy now!"

His fingers working at the buckle, Greg said, "I'll take no chance with a nervous Colt, ma'am."

"Don't fool yourself! Let it drop . . . All right, lower your other arm. Now line out down the road."

He picked up reins, gently touched the bay into motion. He heard her move in behind him and he asked over his shoulder, "You going to leave my Colt laying in the dirt back there?"

"A rider will find it and bring it to the house. Worry more about your health, Mr.—Mr.—? Who are you?"

"Greg Corwin, newly come to Sioux Valley and sort of wondering now why I did."

"Drifter! You said you weren't."

"I just bought Tumbling T from Hobe Terrall."

He could feel the shock of her surprise. "Liar!"

"Like I said, I talk to Mr. Edwards."

He rode slowly on, aware of the woman a few yards behind him as the crawling skin between his shoulder blades seemed aware of the gun she held on him. They came out into the valley, much larger than any Greg had seen before. The road made a cinnamon brown line across rich graze to a wide scattering of corrals, pens and buildings, the largest the ranch house itself. Greg knew a spread this large spelled power.

He rode on at a deliberate pace, the girl somewhere close behind him. His eyes took in the distant ranch, judging its wealth. Now he could see the bunkhouse, a long low structure twice the size of Tumbling T's. They had traveled about halfway across the valley when they were spotted by men working in a corral. They climbed to the top rail and stared.

Diana Edwards ordered, "Ride into the yard, drifter, to the front of the house. Keep your seat in the saddle until you're told to dismount."

"You're sure neighborly!"

"We are—with those we trust. Keep that in mind."

They came into the yard and by now the punchers had abandoned the corral, sauntering up to watch the arrival with wide grins. Greg flushed, checked it and stared stonily over their heads. He rode close to the wide veranda steps and the girl snapped, "Far enough!"

One of the punchers laughed and asked, "What kind of hunting you been doing, Miss Dian'?"

Her voice changed and Greg was surprised by its sudden warmth, though it still held mockery. "Why, Tex, I don't rightly know. Can you guess?"

"Range critter of some sort. No fangs, though."

"Left his gun and belt back on the road."

29

The ranch-house door banged open and a man crossed the wide porch with firm, heavy tread and stood balanced at the top of the steps. Greg instantly sensed authority in the muscular, thick body and the strong legs, slightly spread.

Black eyes swiftly burned over Greg, taking him in with a single glance, and then moved beyond him. "Who's this, Diana?"

Greg said, "I'm—"

"Shut up."

Greg galvanized upright in anger. The man on the porch glared but dancing lights back in the dark eyes enjoyed this meaningless challenge. Diana suddenly appeared to Greg's left, afoot now. She walked with a swinging, feminine grace that held the eye to every line of her body. She ascended the steps and stood beside the man.

"He calls himself Greg Corwin. I caught him riding this way on the ranch road. Claims he's not looking for work. He wore a gun but I made him shuck it into the road."

"Gunhawk? Hired by some of our friends in the valley?"

Greg crossed his hands on the saddlehorn. "Before I answer . . . who are you?"

"Bart Yates. I'm the foreman here. Now, who are you?"

"I'll talk to Vale Edwards. No use talking to a hired hand."

Yates' heavy, handsome face darkened and his hand half lifted to his holster, then dropped away as full lips peeled back in a tight grin.

"You need the sand taken out of you! Tex, hold your gun on him. Rod—Bill—Ed, saddle up. Take this jasper back down the road. It don't matter whether he rides, walks or you rope-drag him. At the ranch line, kick him on his way. Hard!"

A Colt blurred as it lined on Greg and three of the men turned on their heels to run to the corral.

V

Greg leaned forward in the saddle. "Yates, you're quick to order others to do your work. Can't you do it yourself?"

The three men swung around and Tex' gun muzzle lifted in menace. Yates' Colt fairly blurred into his hand. "Tex, saddle my grullah. The rest of you get back to work."

The girl said, "Bart, maybe we'd better find out what he wants."

"Don't bother," Greg said shortly. "Vale Edwards or nobody."

Yates demanded, "Why Vale? Were you paid to shoot him down?"

"I belong to no one but myself."

"Bart, he says he owns Tumbling T." Diana Edwards tugged at Yates' sleeve.

"Tumbling T! But Hobe Terrall—"

"Sold out to me yesterday. He told me nothing about what's going on in Sioux Valley. That's why I want to see Edwards."

Yates balanced at the top of the steps, glared at Tex and the other riders and then signalled them away. They moved

31

off around the corner of the ranch house. Yates turned to Greg. "Where's Terrall?"

"Rode off before I could learn the facts and back down on the sale."

Greg became aware of Diana Edwards. There was something disturbing in her eyes, something speculative and pleased. Greg had to pull his attention from her slim figure back to Yates. She said, "Maybe Dad had better see him, Bart."

Yates shrugged. "All right, Corwin. Maybe we made a mistake—and you'd better hope to God we have. Come inside."

He turned on his heel and strode back across the porch, Diana following after him. Greg swung out of the saddle and turned to ascend the steps. Diana Edwards waited, framed seductively in the dark doorway. "Come in, Mr. Corwin."

He smiled, took off his hat, crossed the porch and stepped into a great, airy room that extended the full front of the house. Dark oak beams supported the ceiling and the walls had been smoothly plastered a dull white, against which buffalo and cougar heads, Indian blankets and shields made a colorful pattern. The furniture was solid and a dark contrast to the bright light streaming in the many windows.

A tall, round-shouldered man with iron gray hair pulled himself slowly and with evident pain from a tufted leather chair near one of the windows. His face was deeply lined from flaunting hawk nose to a slash of pain-twisted lips. The blue eyes, like Diana's, were clear, sharp and shrewd. Yates indicated Greg with a flip of the hand, speaking his name.

Edwards took a hobble step forward and extended his gnarled hand. "Welcome to Bar Y, sir. Is it true you bought Tumbling T?"

Greg accepted the twisted, arthritic hand and knew surprise at the strength of the man's grip. He dropped into the nearby chair Edwards indicated and the old man eased painfully down into his own. "A hell of a way for a cowman to be! But—I asked about Tumbling T."

"Yes, sir, I bought it."

"How much?" Yates snapped. "We offered a fair price and Terrall said he'd take it."

"He sold to me—and I paid a lot more'n you offered. I though *I* had a fair deal."

"You don't know land values up here."

"And I didn't know there was range trouble. That's why I'm here."

Diana had moved behind her father's chair to lean against the back, distracting Greg's attention. Yates looked at the girl, at Greg and back at her and his black eyes grew narrow and mean.

Edwards held Greg's attention. "There has been trouble lately, Mr. Corwin. Our neighbors are suddenly enemies. That's why I try to buy out some of those who'd holster their guns for the right price."

"Right price . . . for Terrall?"

"More than fair!" Yates cut in.

Diana shifted slightly and Greg became aware of her slim, denim-clad hips and legs. He pulled his eyes to her father's pain-grooved face. "I don't know enough to auger with any of you, Mr. Edwards. I found Tumbling T at a price that made me jump at it. Later, I knew why. I run on a bushwhack—riflemen after a woman. Amanda Zane, she told me."

"Rocking Chair!" Edwards exclaimed and threw a knowing look at Yates. "Bart, they're fighting among themselves."

Diana Edwards suddenly grew still at the mention of Amanda and she studied Greg with a new, veiled expression. Her lips held a faint, thoughtful purse. Edwards asked Greg, "Who were the bushwhackers?"

"Don't know. They lined out when I took a hand and I didn't have a look at them. She swore they were Bar Y."

"That's ridiculous! We don't hire gunmen. Ask Bart."

"I don't know enough to know who tells truth or who's against who. All I know is I bought into the middle of something. I'm going to read my brand, though it's plain enough. All my money is tied up in Tumbling T."

"We'll buy you out," Yates offered.

"And I'd lose half what I paid. No, thanks, not if I can help it. That'd just lose my last chance to be something. I don't want to get in any range war. I'm peaceful by nature and, besides, a range war would break me certain. I won't line up with gunhawks—small ones or big ones."

"Maybe you'll have to."

"All I ask is to be left alone. I won't take sides against you —or for you, either. I'll do all I can to be neighborly. I promise it." His voice deepened. "I won't ride an inch or spend a bullet helping you against someone else."

Yates leaned forward, handsome face hawklike. "But you would help others—"

"Against you? No. I'm going to tell them exactly what I told you. If you're fighting them, or they're pushing you— whichever—Tumbling T will take no part or hand."

"How about Rocking Chair?" Diana asked suddenly.

Her question and tone surprised Greg but he demanded, "How's Rocking Chair different except I met Amanda Zane?"

Diana didn't answer, merely watched Greg as Yates said, "Why should we believe you?"

Vale Edwards shifted painfully. "Wait a minute, Bart. Maybe we should. As it stands, we have to watch 'em all. If Corwin keeps his word, that's one stretch of our boundary we won't have to watch. Beef won't disappear in that direction."

Greg asked, "You've lost beef?"

Yates swung around. "Plenty of it and we aim to stop it —buy up baling-wire spreads around us is one way. Use guns to check trouble on our range is another."

34

"How about the sheriff?"

"Sioux Valley's big. So we protect ourselves. The little spreads have gone together to break Bar Y by driving off beef, burning line shacks—that's happened to us. If we're forced to sell, the Terralls, Zanes and Ralls could divide our range between 'em and have a rich graze for a quarter of what it's worth."

Greg had never heard of such a situation but it could happen. On the other hand, Amanda Zane and Cal Weber had told a different story of harassment by Bar Y. Someone lied. The question was—who? Those hidden rifles yesterday —Bar Y as Amanda Zane said? Greg looked at Vale Edwards and had his doubts.

Edwards said, "Corwin, I'll gamble on your word. You'll have no trouble from Bar Y so long as we know we're having no trouble from you. But Bart and our riders will keep an eye on you until we're sure that if you ain't a friend, you're not an enemy."

"That's all I asked."

"Point is you got other neighbors that might figure if you ain't for them, you're against 'em. How will you handle them?"

"I don't know, other than talk straight as I have to you."

"Good luck to you. Bart, we're forgetting our manners. Here's a new neighbor and we can at least wish him well. Get the whiskey."

Yates stood a split second, every line of his body a protest, then he moved across the room to a cabinet and returned with bottle and glasses. Diana left her position behind her father's chair and gave Greg a smile as she sat down on a tapestried sofa nearby. Yates placed the bottle and glasses on a small table near Edwards' chair and the old man poured three drinks.

Greg accepted his, lifted it in response to Edwards "Welcome to Sioux Valley."

Yates barely tasted his, standing to one side, watching—Diana as much as Greg. Edwards asked how Greg had happened to come to Sioux Valley and Greg told the story of his dream and the poker game. Edwards looked at Diana and then at his foreman. "You see! I've always said Sioux Valley could be a paradise."

Yates growled, "Trouble is, no angels settled here."

Greg pulled himself out of the chair and thanked Edwards for the talk and the drink. Edwards extended his twisted hand. "There's an old saying about actions and words. You can bet I'll go by that."

Greg nodded and spoke courteously to Diana. "It was a pleasure meeting you, ma'am."

She laughed provocatively. "The next time I promise to be a lady."

"You are that—even with a Colt in your hand."

Greg turned to Yates. "There's just me and old Cal Weber on Tumbling T now. You're free to run our range if Bar Y beef strays that way. They won't be lost or their brands vented."

Yates turned on his heel and followed Greg out onto the porch. Greg's bay waited at the foot of the steps. He gathered up the reins and started to mount but Yates touched his shoulder. Greg swung around.

The foreman studied him with pursed lips and eyes like black granite. "You talk good, Corwin. I like to hear it."

"Thanks. I meant it."

"That's something for me to learn, ain't it? The old man's stove up. He can't work the range or see everything that's going on. That's my job."

"Meaning?"

"He made the deal with you. I don't say he's right. I don't say he's wrong. But me, I'll keep a sharp eye and loaded gun your way. You're a drifter—no matter how much money you won. You'll be like the rest. The more you look

36

at Bar Y range and beef, the hungrier you'll get. I don't expect you to keep your word for very long. I could be wrong, so you'll get the benefit of the doubt. Toe the line and you'll be all right. But I'll be one jump ahead of you. If you even think of changing your mind, you'll be out of Sioux Valley or planted six feet under it."

Greg choked back dislike for the man and his arrogance. "That's fair enough. But there's another side. Don't you go over the line Edwards and me drew."

He turned to the horse. Yates glared up at him. "While we're swapping promises and threats, I might as well get in another. Stay on Tumbling T. Don't get sociable over here because of what happened."

"I said my piece and have no reason to come back."

"Keep it that way. When I look out for Vale, I look out for his daughter, too. She's over the line for you."

Greg jerked leg and stirrup free of the strong grip. He gave in to an angry urge to deflate the man's assurance and ego. "Point is, does she agree? Have you given that a thought?"

He reined about, set spurs and galloped out of the yard, heading for the pass through the hills. He knew that Barton Yates stood immobile behind him.

VI

Greg checked the bay's defiant gallop, not wanting Yates to think he had thrown a challenge and then fled. Some distance out along the road leading to the pass, he gently touched spurs, setting the bay to an easy trot.

He half hoped Yates might come after him but, as quickly as the thought came, he dismissed it. He had come for peace, not war. He felt he could afford the slight discomfort of stung pride considering the concession he had gained from Vale Edwards.

That brought a vivid memory picture of the daughter leaning on the back of her father's chair, disturbing blue eyes considering him with that peculiar veiled expression, the light from the window behind her making an aura of her red hair. He recalled her lithe figure and long, shapely legs in the form-fitting levis. Suddenly he remembered her question about Amanda Zane and he frowned, sensing some subtle meaning behind it he had missed.

Now almost to the mouth of the pass, he felt free to look back down the slope toward the distant ranch. He could not distinguish the minute figures back there, but guessed that the one near the fence was Yates and the one on the porch might be Diana. He straightened, urged the horse at a faster trot into the pass. He didn't really blame Yates, come to think of it. Diana Edwards probably had every man in the Valley looking long and hard at her one time or another.

Greg dismissed her from his mind but a second later saw Amanda Zane's dark, flashing eyes and almost felt the pressure of her slender body within his arm as, in memory, they rode-double away from the ambush. Amanda—Diana—how different could two women be? He shrugged. What difference did it make? Diana was Yates' property, to hear him tell it, and Amanda Zane strongly hinted of trouble at this point.

A metallic glitter in the road drove both women from his mind. He dismounted and picked up his gunbelt that Diana Edwards had forced him to drop. He buckled it about his waist, pulled the Colt from the holster and examined it. Only the belt and the holster had taken the road dust. There was not so much as a speck in the mechanism of the gun. He slid it back into the holster, mounted and set an easy pace down the winding road.

Beyond the hills, he came onto the main valley road, followed along it until he came to the Tumbling T sign. He drew rein, looked back the way he had come, seeing Yates and Vale Edwards again. His tawny eyes, hard for the moment, returned to the sign. Perhaps his name never would replace Hobe Terrall's? With a growling sound, he turned the bay into the ranch road.

Cal Weber came up as Greg rode into the yard. The old man was bursting with questions but Greg deferred answers until, the bay stabled, the two men went into the ranch house kitchen. Cal slapped mugs on the table by the window and Greg dropped into a chair as the old man poured coffee from a huge granite pot. He sat down, watched Greg sip at the hot brew and at last exploded, "How long you gonna sit there? You've been up to something and I'd guess at Bar Y."

"I made a deal with Vale Edwards."

Cal spewed coffee then glared. "Sold out! You mean to say—?"

"I didn't sell out. So far as Bar Y is concerned, we stay on peaceful here. They won't bother us."

"If you throwed in with them, they'd better send gunhawks over to keep the rest of the valley off us."

Greg told Cal about the arrangement he had made. Cal listened, stiff with anger until his body slowly relaxed and his expression changed to one of uncertain suspicion. He shook his head from time to time but Greg finished the story and waited.

Cal swiped his hand across his lips, tugged at them, and finally spoke, groping for each word. "Fact is, I don't know what to say. For one thing, I don't know you very well. But I know Vale Edwards! Bart Yates has been around long enough that I can plainly read his brand."

"You don't think they'll keep their word?"

Cal took refuge in a deep swig of coffee but said at last, "Depends. They ain't likely to let up on Tumbling T unless you offered something that'd make 'em hold off for a while." He sought help from Greg, found none. "Damn it! No one makes a deal with Bart Yates. A man either sells out or throws in with him. So your big talk last night comes down to getting on the good side of Yates. Nothing more! Ain't that right?"

Greg flushed, then he understood. "Like you said, you don't know me so I give you the right to think I might be saying fine words to cover crooked ones—or to explain 'em."

"How else am I to think? You're a stranger here—a loner against a big outfit. Or against the rest of the Valley *and* Bar Y, the way I think you see it. I don't blame you for look-

40

ing to the strongest side. Point is, I won't work in any way for Bart Yates."

"Cal, I'm not afraid any more'n I got a right to be with guns pointing at me from all directions. You said I had two chances, both of 'em bad. Fighting Bar Y means I lose my hide along with the ranch. Selling out at Bar Y price is a little better, but not much. So I come up with the third way that gives me a chance—stay away from either side. Vale Edwards is going along. I hope the other side does."

"Yates—what'd he say?"

"Took Edwards' orders." Greg grinned. "But didn't like it. Told me to stay away from Bar Y . . . and Diana Edwards."

"So that's how it figures! You saw her? . . . Hard woman to stay away from for a man young and randy like you'll be."

"I think I can manage."

Cal sobered. "They could be tricking you."

"That's what they thought I might be doing to them. I told 'em to wait and see. And that's exactly—so far as Bar Y is concerned—what I have to do."

Cal refilled the mugs, worked at his coffee as he looked distantly out the window. Finally he said, "All you've done makes sense. But why didn't they make the same deal with Hobe?"

"They might've. But, say, I went to 'em instead of breaking into a scared sweat. Cal, I'd guess Bar Y's afraid, too."

"Of what!"

"They said line shacks had been burned and cattle run off, and they're afraid of gunhawks."

"Why, that'd be the Ralls and the Zanes and Hobe—all the rest of 'em. I don't believe it."

"Reckon Sioux Valley folks are just born scared and suspicious?"

"Beats me. Damned if it don't!" Cal chewed at his lip

41

again and then reluctantly decided, "Sounds like both sides are scared of each other for no reason but loose talk, and that happened maybe strange and accidental. But does Bart Yates look like a man who'd lose his nerve?"

"Well . . . no."

"Big as Bar Y is, can you figure any small spread like us going after it?"

"Not alone. But—together? How else do you explain what happened to Bar Y?"

"I don't. Even more, I don't believe it. Take old man Zane for instance. Honest as they come. His daughter's a hell-kitty but she's just as honest. They wouldn't throw in with their neighbors just to rob Bar Y."

"Not rob—but drive out? It'd be a lot of range to divide among 'em."

"No—though it makes sense the way you line it out. You trust them at Bar Y?"

"Yes, though Yates got me a little sandy. But on the other hand, have you liked every honest man you've met?"

Cal gathered up the mugs. He stood a moment looking down at Greg and then turned to the sink with its hand pump. He spoke over the splash of water in the mugs. "Can't argue with or against you. So I'll string along until we can see a sure trail." He wheeled about, leathery face tight. "But the main point is you. If trouble comes from either side—"

"I'll stand up to it. Did you figure I'd run?"

"Felt you wouldn't but wanted you to say it out loud." Cal dried the wet mugs, placed them bottom up on a shelf. "So, palaver's over and we get down to ranching. What do you want me to do tomorrow?"

"You do what's needed for now. I haven't registered the sale and deed with the Recorder. I'd better make Tumbling T legally mine before I start worrying about it."

"And keep your Colt ready, the way things are going."

42

"Come to think of it, Cal, better follow your own advice. A bushwhacker would like to notch a gun for a tophand foreman . . . that is, when we get to full crew."

Cal started to say something but then only nodded and turned to the door. He walked with a firmer stride, his rounded shoulders a little straighter than a moment before.

Early the next morning, Greg saddled and rode out of the ranch yard, leaving Cal mending the barn fence. The sun was dawn-golden and the air crisp, no clouds in the sky. It looked like a day in which no trouble could happen and Greg softly whistled as the bay broke into a gallop. He let the animal work off its energy and then firmly pulled it down to an easy trot. As he passed the Bar Y road, he looked off to where it plunged into the hills. He thought of yesterday's meeting with the feeling Vale Edwards would abide by the understanding they had reached. Then, thinking of Diana, Greg had a fleeting regret that the understanding did not extend to socializing. Well . . . win a little and lose a little, and the win looked big right now.

The hills cut across the road and Greg rode into the pass. He recalled Cal's warning and he sharply searched along the slopes extending back from either side of the road. The pass here was shallow and wide, more a swale than a canyon.

He soon rode into another wide, grassy valley. Ahead, he could see a line of trees crowning another range of low hills, making a dark green barricade in the distance. Hobe Terrall had said the town lay beyond. Greg's whistle broke out again. On a morning like this, he'd let trouble find him if it dared challenge this bright sun and sharp, invigorating air.

As he approached the trees, he caught a flicker of movement. A moment later a rider broke out into sunlight, riding toward him. Greg's right hand dropped to his side, fingers brushing the leather of his holster. He did not slacken the bay's stride. The approaching rider sat tall and straight and Greg suddenly realized that this tense, suspicious meeting

43

of a stranger typified the situation in Sioux Valley. Yates had been right when he said no angels lived in this paradise.

Closer now, Greg saw a slender man about mid-thirties, with a wiry body, face shaded by a battered Stetson brim. They were within a few yards of one another and Greg caught the suspicious gleam of narrowed eyes, and angular jaw and slash of a mouth below a long, straight nose.

Greg gave a courteous nod. "Howdy."

The man spoke the single word in return, thin lips barely moving, eyes searching gimlets. They passed and Greg's lips moved wryly. They had been like two dogs, sidling about one another with fangs half-exposed.

"Hey!"

Greg started at the hail from behind him and he looked back. The man had turned about. "Ain't you the new owner of Tumbling T? . . . Thought so. I'm Hal Stern, foreman of Anchor."

Greg rode back, pulled in beside the man. Stern offered his hand, suspicion gone and his thin lips forming an equally thin smile. "We ain't exactly neighbors, Anchor being at the far end of the valley, but we got things in common. You'll be welcome at Anchor any time."

"Thanks. I'll get down that way as soon as I can. But how did you know I bought Tumbling T?"

"'Manda Zane. Saw her yesterday on my way into Redman. She says you're pretty good with a rifle."

"Oh, she told you about—"

"How you drove off those Bar Y killers."

"I don't know who they were. For that matter, even Miss Zane didn't see them."

"Hell, who else could it be!" Stern did not wait for reply. "Hobe Terrall never had sand enough to take a hand like you did. The more there are ready to stand up to Bar Y, the better Sioux Valley will be. You come see us, Corwin. I can

44

speak for Sam Ralls—he owns Anchor. Come any time. Hear?"

Stern flipped his hand as he reined his horse about, leaving Greg with his protest unspoken. He watched Stern ride off. Greg had an impulse to call him back but then decided it would be better to state his position to the rancher rather than the foreman. Greg thoughtfully resumed his journey to Redman.

VII

———◆•◆———

Greg's first sight of Redman at a distance surprised him. A white church spire lifted above the trees that shaded a town that sat in the middle of a wide valley. Greg, sitting the bay on the crest of a low hill, could trace the dirt roads converging on it like wheel spokes to the hub. He had thought to see the usual scabruous cowtown, a human excresence of weather-beaten buildings with peeling paint or whitewash, false fronts sometimes askew as the structures settled to corner or side.

But when he rode into Redman, he saw structures of solidity and substance, from the small houses on the outskirts to the brick bank building and the county courthouse in the small town square, lined with hitchracks and filled with passing buggies and buckboards.

A bit overwhelmed, Greg allowed the bay to drift with the flow, finally turning in at a rack before one of the many saloons. He dismounted, tied the reins and turned to look down the line of buildings, surveying all of the square that he could see. Then he studied the structure directly before him.

He did not need to read the sign, RANCHER'S REST or to enter the place to know its clientele and its status in Redman. He noted the heavy maroon drapes covering the windows and hiding the interior, and the ornate glass in the double doors with the twin, brightly polished knobs. No batwings—and that alone proclaimed the Rancher's Rest a nearly private club rather than saloon.

He abruptly circled the hitchrack, crossed the street and strode up a planked walk to the courthouse. After a few inquiries, he found his way to a narrow door in a basement corridor and stepped up to a long counter. A portly man, wearing black dustguards on his shirt sleeves, looked up from a rolltop desk and asked his business.

Quick interest replaced bored suspicion when Greg produced abstract, bill of sale and authorization for transfer of title to Tumbling T. The man studied the documents, pausing here and there with an occasional slanted look up under shaggy gray brows at Greg. Finally he said in a noncommital tone, "I didn't figure Hobe would sell out to someone like you."

"It just happened. I was looking around to buy most any spread. Made a deal on this one."

"That'll make someone I know unhappy. Aim to resell or ranch it?"

"Considering the price I paid, ranch it."

"You know, then. Too bad you didn't look and ask around first. Might even have trouble ranching it, considering the way things're going."

Greg pulled out a gold piece and placed it on the counter. "Register the deed, friend, and I'll take care of my own tangled rope."

"No harm meant. Just trying to be friendly."

"No offense taken. And Vale Edwards said he'd be neighborly, too."

47

"Vale? . . . Well . . . that's different. This'll take a little time. When'll you pick up the registration certificate?"

"Hour?—or two? I'll look around Redman."

"Best saloon's the Rancher's Rest." The man fingered the legal papers. "Trades with your kind of folks."

Leaving the building, Greg paused in its shadow and slowly studied the three sides of the square in his view. The town looked busy and prosperous, and that always indicated the prosperity of the country round about, Greg knew. Yet there was an invisible cloud gathering against the clear blue sky above, a cloud slowly being shaped by the greed of men. It subtly dulled the bright glow of the sunshine.

Greg's lips flattened. He hitched at his gunbelt and strode away down the planked walk, crossed the street and slowly moved along the line of stores. His stroll was not entirely aimless. He noted the names and businesses, from barber-shop to saddlery, merchants with whom he'd have to deal. He didn't enter a store, leaving that for a later time when he would need supplies.

He turned toward a saloon, about to go in, but remembered his own status was changing right this moment over there in the Recorder's office. He strolled on, circling the square and coming again to the Rancher's Rest.

After a perceptible hesitation, he climbed the steps, crossed the narrow clean-swept porch under the canopy, and opened the ornate door. He entered a large, cool room. He instantly became aware that he walked on carpet instead of sawdust. The tables were well spaced about the area before a comparatively small, richly carved bar. He had no sense of the cramped, cluttered, shabby areas of other saloons.

Heavy fixtures hung from the ceiling bearing ornate lamps. Mirrors gleamed from within heavy gilded frames lining the walls that were covered with a red, gold-tracery

48

cloth. Greg involuntarily blinked at such luxury as his gaze swept around the room.

"Looking for someone, cowboy?"

Greg wheeled to the bar and the man behind it. Here was barkeeper such as Greg had always known them; the same florid and full cheeks, smoothly combed hair and the little forelock plastered just above the brow. But there it ended. This one wore a spotless white shirt, silk string tie and a buttoned vest, smoothly dark, looped across with a gold watch chain bearing a lodge charm.

"A drink," Greg answered.

"Not here. You belong at one of the places down the street."

"My money's as good as the next one's."

"Sure, the money's all right. But here we like to know who spends it." The man's hard eyes faintly softened. "Cowboy, you've seen places like this before. You have to own at least one acre and one cow before you even look in the door. The closer you get to the bar, the more land and beef you need. Not that *I* give a damn, but the customers like the idea."

Greg leaned against the bar. "Is the whiskey or beer any better'n down the street?"

The man frowned and his pudgy hand dropped below the bar. "Just giving you tips and advice, friendly like. Let's keep it that way and forget the questions?"

"I'd like to know who I'm going to trade with and the kind of goods I'll get."

Uncertainty flicked across the man's face but he quickly judged Greg's faded shirt, searched his face for some subtle sign. His lips pursed stubbornly. "Okay, I'll say it again—the last time before I come over on your side with a bung starter. The sign says, 'Rancher's Rest,' and that don't mean drifting punchers."

"Do I have to show abstract or brand registration? I own Tumbling T."

49

"Be damned if you—! Oh—oh, I heard Hobe Terrall sold out! But Bar Y . . ."

"I bought it."

The bartender's hand came in sight and his florid face grew redder. He couldn't quite meet Greg's eyes. "Sorry—damn' sorry, mister—mister . . . ?"

"Corwin, Greg Corwin. Of course, I could get the Recorder across the street if I need vouching—"

"Not at all, Mr. Corwin. You're right welcome! And all your drinks this time are on the house. I'm Mike Lafferty. I'd be hoping you really understand I have to be careful here."

"You didn't tell me if the drinks are better, Lafferty."

The man whipped about, lifted bottle from the mirror shelf, poured a drink and offered it to Greg. "Try for yourself, Mr. Corwin. The best in all Sioux Valley if not the whole Territory. Would you be having a table? I'd glad bring a bottle over."

Greg, smothering a grin, gravely sampled the drink, looked uncertain a moment as Lafferty seemed to hold his breath, blue eyes rounded. Greg finally nodded. "It'll do, Mike, and I'm pleased to meet you. No table. I'll stand up to my drinks, thank you."

Lafferty breathed again. Greg nursed his drink, the bartender hovering near. Greg asked questions about the Valley, Lafferty quickly answering. Then Greg recalled the rider he had met. "What about Hal Stern, other than he's Anchor foreman?"

"I know Hal, though he doesn't come in here much. Sam Ralls, his boss, does. Hal's a hard working coot, from all I hear. Always dreaming big. Dead set to own a ranch some-day—says something like Anchor. Or, maybe, ramrod a big outfit like Bar Y."

"I hear that's ramrodded pretty fair right now."

"Yep. Bart Yates. You'll see him in here from time to time. Vale Edwards used to come regular, but he's stove up."

"What about Rocking Chair?"

Lafferty studied Greg a moment from under his brows. "You know considerable about the Valley right now, seems like."

"I've ridden around—and listened."

"Well . . . maybe I shouldn't talk. But you'll learn sooner or later. Rocking Chair—the Zanes—the old man and that girl."

"Don't think much of 'em?"

"I didn't say that. But an accident happened out that way —to the old man. They had an idea Bart Yates caused it, though God knows why that popped into their heads! He proved he was miles away."

"What kind of accident?"

Lafferty swiped the bar. "Old Man Zane flushed a drifting beef killer, I guess, and took a slug. Crippled him up. But that ain't the point, Mr. Corwin."

"What is?"

"You—and how you'll get along. Sioux Valley ain't happy these days. The real sore spot is Rocking Chair—stirring up trouble all they can. They'll try to pull you into it soon's they know you bought out Hobe Terrall. Take some advice? though it ain't my place to give it."

"Depends."

"Just listen to Amanda—that's the daughter—but don't do anything about it. Them and Bar Y ain't friendly and your spread's right between 'em."

Lafferty started to explain further but his eyes lifted beyond Greg as the door opened and closed. The bartender gave Greg a meaningful look, moved to another position and said, "Howdy, Mr. Unger."

"A good day, Mike. It matches that good liquor of yours. I'll take a sample."

Greg had a first impression of a dark face, all jaw and harsh angles until the man smiled—it transformed him. He

51

spoke with easy courtesy. "Mike, another sample for the gentleman. With your permission, of course, sir."

Greg, caught momentarily off balance, automatically nodded and the man's teeth flashed in a widening smile. "Good! His brand, Mike. My pleasure, sir. I'm Fred Unger. I run the Redman bank, down at the corner."

He extended his hand. Strong, wiry fingers wrapped around Greg's with steel power, exerted for a second and then released. Greg introduced himself and Unger indicated the drinks Lafferty had brought. "Your health, sir."

Greg acknowledged with a lift of his glass. Unger studied Greg with frank curiosity. "You're new in Sioux Valley, sir. Beef buying over this way, by chance, or looking for breed stock?"

"No. Matter of fact, I was looking to buy a ranch."

"Indeed! Now that might be hard."

"Not very. I bought it. Tumbling T."

"Hobe Terrall's spread!" His evident surprise did not hit a true note, but the thought flicked in and out of Greg's mind. "Well, Mr. Corwin, one of us!"

"Might be . . . in a way."

Unger's deep-sunken, dark eyes sharpened a second. "How about a table, Mr. Corwin? We should get acquainted —rancher and banker. Mike! Bring a bottle over, will you? I think I prefer Mr. Corwin's brand."

He led the way to a table well away from the bar. Greg followed, quite aware of the subtle compliment the banker had paid to his whiskey taste. His first impressions of the man moved from liking to suspicion and back to liking again. Unger's smile could charm a knot out of a fence post but somehow, surrounded as the smile was by long jaw and hard bone, it didn't quite come through.

Lafferty brought bottle and glasses and again Unger poured. He lifted his glass. "To Tumbling T and its new owner, sir!"

A moment later, with a glance toward Lafferty behind the distant bar, he grew sober and his voice lowered. "I take it, Corwin, you thoroughly sized up Sioux Valley before you bought Tumbling T?"

"As a matter of fact, I didn't—"

"But you have by now, I take it?"

"Yes . . . by now."

Unger sadly shook his head and his cavernous eyes grew compassionate. "Too bad, sir. I wish you had come to me. I could have told you a few things."

"Like Bar Y?—and Amanda Zane? the little spreads against the big one?"

"Well . . . it's not as bad as you make it sound. Tumbling T is a good ranch, understand. One of the better ones. But the chance of it staying that way, considering conditions around here . . . I'm sure you understand me."

"You'd have advised me not to buy?"

"Perhaps, but at a very low price. May I ask what you did pay?"

"Do you know what Bar Y offered? . . . Well, twice that."

The banker's hand slapped angrily down on the table. "And if I know Bar Y, you'll end up selling to them at *their* price. I know what's happened to Vale Edwards but that's no excuse to let Bart Yates ride wild and hard and wide without a check rein. Is that the way you size it up, Mr. Corwin?"

"I've heard plenty. Might be. But I'll have to find out for myself."

"By then you'll be dead—or broke. I'm speaking quite openly, though I can't quite understand why I should to a stranger. Perhaps because I like your looks . . . maybe the way you talk . . . something. Let me ask, how long can you hold your breath financially? I mean—two, three years without selling beef?"

53

"Why should I do that? Railhead's just over the mountains and it's a good driving trail, I'm told."

Unger's lips peeled in a slow, wry smile. "Were you also told Bar Y can cut off the trail and probably will if they want Tumbling T badly enough?"

"No."

"They can, I assure you."

Greg slowly circled his shot glass between thumb and fingers as, underbrow, he studied the sincere, dark face across the table. He suddenly shot the question, "Does Bar Y do business with you?"

He did not miss the swiftly checked flush that started up out of the man's wing collar. But Unger's shrug dismissed suspicion. "A bit, naturally. But I don't grow rich on it. I'd be broke if Sioux Valley was a one-ranch area. I make mortgage loans on land sales or on next year's beef sales. I loan money so men like you can buy equipment or breeding stock. Where would I be with just one big, rich ranch that wouldn't need any of that service?"

"Nowhere, I reckon."

"Exactly! So I certainly don't like what Bar Y is doing."

Greg finished his drink and Unger instantly filled the shot glass again, though Greg tried to protest. Unger laughed. "Next time, you'll buy the drinks, if that bothers you. A banker always gets his money back, one way or another."

"So I figure," Greg answered dryly, lifted the glass to Unger and sipped. "So, I wonder what you're trying to tell me—out of friendship, of course."

Unger looked doleful. "Corwin, you hurt my feelings! I assure you . . . Oh, well, I guess I understand. I'm a man of impulse. You wouldn't know that. I take a quick liking sometimes, even beyond business and—sometimes—I get in trouble because of it."

"No trouble. Just wondering—friendship? or business? or both?"

Unger sighed, then leaned forward again. "Both, say. You know what the situation is here. Did you ever gamble, Mr. Corwin?"

"Now *that* I've done!"

"All right. Then say I'm doing a little careful gambling in Sioux Valley. I think Bar Y's going to gobble up everything in sight, one way or another. The ranchers won't have much of a chance against Bar Y pressure and . . ." His voice lowered ominously. ". . . Guns. That's bound to come sooner or later, for I've been through range wars elsewhere and I know."

"Why do you gamble if you're so certain—?"

"It'll work that way? It will!" Unger smiled and shrewdly placed his finger beside his nose. "Bar Y can drive you off, say, or the Zanes, or Sam Rall. But what would they do against a bank?"

"You'd take a bullet as quick as the next one, I'd guess."

"True, but then what? The bank is a corporation, friend. Shoot me, there'd be another president—and another."

"So?"

"So the bank would like to buy up some of these small spreads on the quiet."

"Quiet? How?"

"The Recorder is my friend. He would see to that. Oh, sure, it'd come out in time. But too late, you see. I'd buy up and let the owners stay on and work the beef, sharing profit, if they wanted, until Bar Y got too hot for them to stay. Bar Y would be blocked and the bank'd be in business. We could sell the spreads at a profit to Bar Y or anybody else if we didn't want to hold 'em. It's a gamble, like I said, but careful."

Greg studied the man in uncertain, wry admiration, not fully understanding the ramifications of the plan but sensing it would work. "And you want to buy Tumbling T?"

"Why not? Right now, if you like. Jack Cole can give the

55

bank a deed registration as well as you. It'd be done fast and quiet."

"How much?"

"Ah! Now we become businessmen, Corwin. Much as I like you, I have to think of my bank. I'll top Bar Y's offer but won't meet what you paid Terrall. Say—right down the middle between 'em. And you can work the beef for at least a year—split cost and profit."

"I paid a reasonable price—"

"Right! But for normal times. I know the bind you're in. I'll help you some, but not all sweet charity. Better grab while I'm offering the deal."

Greg's eyes grew distant in thought. This could be a way out. He just might buy a spread elsewhere now, though not as big as Tumbling T. Three faces flashed across his mind. Bart Yates, dark and domineering, gave way to Amanda Zane, fiery, slender and fighting off three hidden riflemen. She, in turn, gave way to Diana Edwards of the rich, provocative figure and enigmatic smile and eyes. The faces vanished in a split second then he heard Cal Weber promising to stay on, to work until round-up despite age and stiffness.

Greg took a deep breath. "Nice offer, Mr. Unger, and one I might've taken yesterday."

"Why not now!"

"I've been to Bar Y. I talked to Bart Yates and I'd guess he just might be what you think he is."

"So's Edwards. They're two of a—"

"Rein in! I talked to Edwards, too. We've made a truce between us. Not a sell-out and I'm not siding Bar Y—just a truce. So, I think I'll hang onto Tumbling T. Thank you just the same."

Unger sat quite still, eyes probing at Greg as though searching for hidden meaning or undisclosed facts. "Think you can trust Edwards?"

"I have to find out, don't I?"

"It might cost you everything. My way—"

"Good offer, Unger. I'm not saying that. I just figure to hang on, keep away from both sides."

Unger started to protest but instead eased back in his seat. "Tomorrow I could change my mind—maybe even in an hour."

"It's your mind and your privilege, Mr. Unger. I guess it's my turn to stand for the drinks."

VIII

On his return from Redman, Greg and Cal made a little ceremony of placing new deed and title registrations in the office safe. Greg locked the steel door and then they had their celebration drink. Greg told the old man about Unger's offer.

"Maybe you should've taken it," Cal said dubiously.

"And disappoint Bar Y—and you?"

"Me?"

"Had to show you I'm staying. And I've been wondering what kind of foreman you'll make. By the way, you're drawing that kind of wage right now."

"Greg, I'm only a bunged-up puncher. Come fall, I just might do a foreman's job. But there's no crew now, so who in hell do I order around! There's only me and—"

"Jump to your own orders, then." Greg sobered and sat down at the desk. "We'd better look things over pretty careful, Cal. How about supplies? What's the first job we ought to do?"

"Well, we need . . ."

Finally, by lamp light, they covered all the immediate

problems. They went to the kitchen for supper, still talking Tumbling T's prospects, Greg gradually firing Cal with a new sense of hope and determination. As they finished coffee, Cal suddenly asked, "Can't really figure why Unger wanted to buy you out."

"He made sense in a way."

"How'd he take your turning him down?"

"He said me and Edwards making peace might mark the beginning of the end of the range trouble. Didn't sound real enthusiastic, though."

"Seeing what he's doing and planning, no reason why he should."

"You're right. By the way, I ran into Hal Stern on the road into town. Invited me over to Anchor any time."

"That's Hal, always friendly. A good man, too."

"Seemed to figure I'd throw in with him, the Zanes and the others."

"They all will. I hope you're as lucky explaining to 'em as you were to Edwards."

For the next three days, Greg rode over various sections of Tumbling T range with Cal. He was familiar with much of it but the old man took him to draws, canyons and little hill meadows that Greg had not seen before. They made a rough tally of the beef, finding it close enough to Hobe's book figure that Greg felt satisfied.

On the last day, they came to the Bar Y line fence and followed it, drifting westward into broken country. Now and then they had to leave the fence when it climbed steep hills or the strong wire and posts blocked draws and canyons. But they would work back to it, only to be forced to detour again.

They circled a tumble of hills and draws and worked their way back along a small canyon to the fence again. The canyon suddenly opened onto another of the small meadows and, ahead, Greg saw the glint of barbed wire. A second later, he abruptly drew rein and pointed ahead. "What happened there!"

A hundred yards of fence was down, only the gaunt posts standing, the wire a tangle of barbed loops. Just beyond, mostly a heap of black ashes and charred uprights, stood the remains of a small structure. The canyon breeze occasionally picked up a handful of black ash, swirled it about for a second and then dropped it.

Cal stared. "Damned if I know. That shack and that fence was standing a month ago. Hobe and me worked this section and I know."

Greg grimly spoke to the horse and moved forward, Cal at his side. Now and then Greg looked down at the ground, searching for signs of riders. He recalled Edwards' claim that Bar Y had been attacked and this seemed to be proof of it. But he found no sign by the time they had come up to the twisted wire that formed an ugly, open barrier between them and the remains of the shack.

"Who could have done this, Cal?"

"Beats me. I know Hobe didn't."

"Zanes?"

"Not Amanda Zane, for one. Sam Ralls wouldn't cross our range to do something like this without telling Hobe what he had in mind."

"Some of the others?"

Cal looked blank. "I don't know. There ain't been no word and something like this'd be bound to come out. You'd figure Bar Y would raise hell all over the valley."

Greg looked along the destroyed fence and then the meadow extending back into Tumbling T range. "Let's spread out. There has to be sign if some of our neighbors did this."

Both men reined about, first paralleling the fence and then circling out into Tumbling T range. Greg moved slowly, searching for even the faintest sign. He worked out and back and came to one end of the cut wire as Cal rode up. The old man shook his head at Greg's questioning look.

Greg said, "And I didn't find any—"

"Greg!"

Cal looked over Greg's shoulder beyond the broken fence. Greg twisted about as two riders came out of a nearby draw on the Bar Y side of the wire. Greg instantly recognized Bart Yates. The other was obviously a Bar Y puncher. Both men came steadily on with an intentness that made both Greg and Cal touch their holsters.

Yates and his man pulled up just beyond the coils of cut wire and Yates said menacingly, "Looking over your work, Corwin?"

Cal started but Greg spoke quickly to check the old man's anger. "This is none of ours."

"Expect me to believe that! Me'n Joe have been watching you for the last quarter hour."

Greg folded his hands on the saddle horn and studied Yates askance. The big man flushed faintly and his jaw firmed in mounting anger. Greg said, "If we did this, do you think we'd be around to let you catch us?"

"You came back to see if we found out. We knew ten days ago. I knew when you soft-talked Vale. In fact, we mentioned it."

"So you did—and so you know I wasn't even in Sioux Valley when this was done. Seems like you keep trying to find fight-talk, Yates."

Greg straightened. "Just now we thought maybe some of our neighbors cut across Tumbling T range without telling us. But there's no sign. We just cut all around for it. Look if you like."

"I looked," Yates answered grudgingly and his big body subtly eased down into the saddle. "Sign's all on our side of the fence. I figure they came across west of here, rode Bar Y range and set the fire."

61

"Why would they cut the fence here?" Greg asked reasonably.

Yates growled, "How do I know the way sneak riders think! Maybe to throw us off. Come to think of it, they'd talk to you before we'd get any hint. Did they?"

"No."

"You're protecting 'em."

"That's like saying I'm lying to you. You keep pushing."

Yates' lips snapped shut like the thin jaws of a trap. "That could be—except Vale was fool enough to hobble me so far as you're concerned. He'll wake up—soon, I hope. But you haven't answered me."

"I told you we knew nothing about this until today. I've been busy minding my own business, picking up the pieces Terrall dropped when he sold me this hunk of trouble range. You'll have to look somewhere else, Yates."

"I will, and don't forget it! While I'm at it, I'll keep an eye on you."

"Do that, friend. There'd be nothing better to prove I'm not taking sides. Let's ride, Cal. We got work to do."

He calmly reined about and rode off, his back to Bart Yates and his rider. He heard Cal move in after him as they crossed the meadow, heading into their own range. As they came to the mouth of a shallow canyon, Cal drew abreast. "He's still back there watching us."

"It'll do him good."

"He's sure randy, that one!"

"He has a right to be, seeing what happened." They entered the canyon and Greg thoughtfully slowed the pace of the bay. "Cal, what's further west of us—where Yates said the fence was cut?"

"Rocking Chair next. Beyond that, Rafter H. Then the mountains bounding the valley."

"This Rafter H—?"

"Bob Hoskins—not him. In fact, he's riding something

62

mighty close to your trail—and has been for sometime. Thrown in with the others but sort of keeps a tight rope on 'em when he can."

"Well, that's maybe one friend I'll find."

"Don't count on it if Bart Yates pushes too hard."

Late that afternoon they came to another Bar Y line shack. It stood unscathed just beyond the fence, empty now but obviously used on occasion. Signs of horses and glitter of empty tin cans some distance out in the grass confirmed a recent visit.

"Looks like the whole crew," Cal commented. "Why are they working this section of their range like it was round-up time?"

"Let's leave Bar Y problems to Bar Y," Greg said dryly, "since we have enough of our own."

They rode a short way beyond and came on a boundary marker set just this side of the Bar Y fence.

"End of Tumbling T range," Cal commented, "that is, on this side of the fence. Bar Y goes on yonderly almost to the end of the valley. Beyond that marker, on this side, is Rocking Chair. Hobe and Zane never put up a fence between 'em. They figured there was no need for it."

"So would I." Greg indicated the fence. "Wish Bar Y would see it that way, too."

"You're wishing for heaven, I'd say."

They turned back from this corner where three ranches adjoined and headed for the distant house. Greg was satisfied with what he had seen of Tumbling T. It met every part of the dream he had of Sioux Valley country except . . . He made a small grimace when he thought of Bart Yates, his rider, and the burned shack and cut fence. A part of a nightmare had slid into the other dream somehow.

The next morning, Greg and Cal started the needed repair of the fence around the ranch yard, replacing posts here and there, restringing wire. It was hot work and, as the sun moved higher, Greg shed his shirt. Muscles rippled along his wide bare shoulders, chest and arms as he labored beside Cal.

Intent on their work, neither was aware of the rider until a shadow fell across them. Greg, holding a new post as Cal filled earth about it, looked up and around.

Amanda Zane sat her saddle, looking down at him. He blinked with surprise and heard Cal's short grunt as Amanda Zane said, "Howdy. Something's come up. We have to talk."

Greg released the post and stepped away, swiping his hand across his sweating forehead. He took the opportunity to look more sharply at her. Shadowed against the sun, he had the impression of a slim yet full silhouette of a woman. She wore levis, washed blue, that clung to her long legs. Soft boots with small toes were thrust into the saddle stirrups.

"Glad to see you, ma'am. But talk about what?"

"Trouble." She gestured over her shoulder back to the road leading to the yard. "I'm not alone but there's no hurrying Bob Hoskins. He and Hal Stern are coming up."

Greg looked beyond her and saw two riders approaching the gate. He turned back to her. "Light down. A visit's welcome."

"This one might not be—for you. But thanks."

He had noticed that she eyed him a bit strangely, a faint shadow of a smile playing about her lips. He suddenly became aware of his bare chest, flushed and whipped about to his shirt lying on the ground. He shrugged into it, fumbling at the buttons.

By now, the two riders had come into the yard and Amanda had dismounted. She looked small now, very feminine and yet far from fragile. She smiled again as Greg fumbled the last shirt button into place. Her eyes veiled a second as though hiding a sudden thought, then she turned quickly away to the two men.

64

Greg recognized Hal Stern. The other man was of medium height and build and Greg saw a round, fleshy face, a bulbous nose set like a circle of dough in its center. His eyes were almost hidden in flesh. His shirt and denims showed signs of hard wear and many washings and the leather of the gunbelt about his thick waist was scuffed and stained. But the Colt in the holster reflected the sun in an oily gleam.

Amanda indicated the two men. "Hal Stern of Anchor and Bob Hoskins of Rafter H. This is Greg Corwin."

Stern grinned and made a faint gesture with his hand. Hoskins' full cheeks quivered as he spoke an acknowledgment. Cal moved up and shot a quick, meaningful glance at Greg who said, "Light and rest your saddles."

Stern and Hoskins dismounted, Hoskins with a series of puffs and grunts. Afoot, he proved to be shorter than Greg had thought, body as round as his face.

Greg led the way to the house, Amanda striding beside him. Greg slanted a look at her. So far, he had seen but two Sioux Valley women but he wondered if all broke the rules of modesty as Amanda and Diana did. Jeans, shirts and boots, sitting saddle like a man! It bothered Greg, used to more decorous clothing and manners. Yet, he thought, some he had seen in the past were not as feminine as the woman who walked beside him. Or as honest, the thought flashed through his mind as he opened the door for Amanda and her friends.

He led the way to the parlor and suggested coffee around. Amanda and Stern shook their heads. Hoskins moistened his lips. "Thank ye, no coffee. But it's been a dry ride."

Greg produced bottle and glasses. Hoskins immediately poured a drink but Hal Stern waved it away. Greg placed bottle and glasses on a table near Hoskins.

"What brings you?" Greg asked.

Amanda's look asked Hoskins and Stern if she should be

spokesman. At their faint nods, she answered, "We hope it's neighborly."

"So do I," Greg agreed.

"By now you've learned how it is in Sioux Valley, but I guess our first meeting made that clear enough. You've been here long enough, Mr. Corwin, that we'd like to know how you stand. We have to—"

"You keep riding in circles," Hal Stern cut in. "I'll come out with it, Corwin. We figured you'd throw in with us small ranchers in the Valley. Now we've heard you're siding with Bar Y."

Greg clamped control on his surprise and asked calmly, "Who said that?"

"I heard it in town."

"Unger?"

Stern said stubbornly, "Just talk around the saloons. We heard you went to Bart Yates and made an agreement with him. You throwed in."

Amanda demanded, "Is that so? Did you go to Bar Y?"

"I went there and I talked to Vale Edwards, not Bart Yates."

The girl almost spat the words. "You're afraid! And you crawled to Bar Y! Do you think that's going to keep Yates from taking you over? You've just played into his hands. Now he's free to hit the rest of us. But he'll turn on you when he's ready."

Greg snapped, "You haven't asked me what I did or what I plan."

Her small fists doubled at her sides, eyes ablaze. Before she could retort, Hoskins said lazily, "I'd kind of like to hear him, 'Manda. Seems only fair. Besides, I'd like another drink before he gets mad at me."

The fat man looked blandly around at them, full shot glass in dimpled fingers. He made a deprecating gesture.

66

"Here we go, shouting and augering and accusing when we've only heard one side."

"I told exactly what I heard," Stern said through set teeth.

Suddenly a new personality appeared in the man, as though from behind a pleasant but concealing curtain. His lips had lifted from his teeth and his brows pulled down as his eyes slitted. Greg had seen such an expression only once when, years before, he had watched a gunslinger pick a fight with a man whom he killed a few moments later.

Hoskins didn't seem to notice the change or, perhaps, he accepted it through familiarity. "As they say in court, Hal, what you heard ain't evidence. I figure Corwin might give us some of that. Agree to be fair, 'Manda?"

She stood undecided, fists still clenched. Slowly, her fingers opened and she looked at Greg. "I'm listening."

Greg told what he had done and why. They listened without interruption but he could see their minds had closed against him. Still he pressed on, trying to make them understand why he should remain neutral. Gradually Amanda subtly lost some of her anger, though she plainly did not agree. Hal Stern sat stiff and obdurate, long fingers beating a soft but angry tattoo on the chair arm.

"So that's the way it is," Greg finished. "I'm a stranger here and I have no quarrel with anybody."

Stern pulled himself up and shoved his hat on his head. "You make it sound reasonable, I'll say that. But the brand reads just like it did before."

Hoskins refilled his glass. "Hal, you're the jumpingest man I ever saw. Makes me tired to watch you. Like what you're thinking now. Me, I'm not so sure I wouldn't try to do what Corwin's doing was I new and got hoodwinked by Hobe Terrall. Now *he's* the one sold out in more ways'n one, if you ask me."

"Thanks," Greg said dryly.

"For what?" Hoskins lifted his glass. "I'm the one to be thanking you."

Amanda Zane stood unmoving, probing eyes moving from Stern to Greg to Hoskins, back to Greg. She took a deep breath. "Mr. Corwin, maybe Bob is right about you."

"It's the way I see it," Greg answered flatly. "I'll fight nobody. Your quarrel's your own and has nothing to do with me."

"Suppose it did?"

"I'll need proof of it."

"If you mean it, come with me."

"Now?"

"Now—unless . . . ?"

He caught the implication and his jaw tightened. "Let me saddle up."

Hoskins sighed regretfully. "Now I got to go riding again. I'd hoped we could sit around jawing and having a drink now and then."

"Help yourself," Greg said shortly.

"Don't know but what I will. 'Manda, you ain't got no need of me. This is mighty good liquor, Corwin."

Greg turned on his heel. Amanda, Stern a step behind her, followed Greg out to the yard. He roped and saddled the bay. Cal gave him a questioning look as Greg led the bay out of the corral. Greg indicated the house and said in a low voice, "The fat one's in there working on our whiskey. If he needs taking care of—"

"Not Bob Hoskins! And don't tally him too low. If there were others like him over the valley, we wouldn't be in trouble."

Greg swung into the saddle and rode out to meet Amanda and Stern. They turned their horses with him and rode out of the yard. Amanda headed toward her Rocking Chair, Greg and Stern slightly behind her. All of them rode in stiff silence for a mile or more, then Stern suddenly expelled his breath.

"Bob's right. I jump. Corwin, I spoke too fast. I hope I'm wrong."

He had suddenly become the man Greg had first met just outside Redman. The Hal Stern in Greg's parlor had completely vanished. "Like Bob said, we can't figure how a stranger will think. We're so spurred by Bar Y, we think everyone understands."

"He will," Amanda threw over her shoulder.

"That's why I figure unless . . . Hell! there I go again—jumping. No hard feelings Corwin? Yet?"

"None . . . yet."

"That's fair enough."

"But suppose," Greg added, "after I see whatever you're showing me, I still think it's not my fight?"

"You won't," Amanda answered shortly.

Stern's dark face tightened. "Here in Sioux Valley, everyone's got a fight, friend. It's come to that. Remember when we learned two and two makes four? Like that here, one side or the other. You're for Bar Y or against Bar Y. You're for us or against us . . . two plus two and you come up with the answer. There's just one right one, ain't there?"

IX

Silence fell on the three riders, though an inward weighing had replaced strain and tension. Greg could sense it. For the first time since his talk with Edward Vale, he felt uncertain of his impression of the crippled man or of Amanda Zane and Hal Stern. The whole situation had become fluid and tricky. That which appeared right became questionable. He could understand why Amanda Zane accused him of fear, why Hal Stern implied he had sold out and lied. Even Cal's wisdom might not be that at all but only a distortion of the situation shaped by Hobe Terrall's fears and pressures. Where, then, lay the straight trail?

Yet Greg couldn't completely distrust Edward Vale. But then he wondered if a painful crippling could warp and twist the inner man as well as the outer. Greg might have looked on exactly the false man Vale wanted him to see while the true man remained hidden. Bart Yates' hiring and continued presence suggested it.

Amanda broke the silence with a surprising question. "What was Vale like when you saw him?"

Greg told her. Hal Stern watched Greg closely, as though

probing deep behind the words, his own expression telling nothing. He looked over at Amanda and spoke tentatively, "Now that don't sound like the man I been hearing about. Do you reckon we've slapped a wrong brand—?"

"No! Look at what he's done. That tells you. Corwin doesn't know, so Vale fooled him. But at the end of this ride he'll find out well enough."

"So he will," Stern sighed.

"Diana Edwards—how was she?" Amanda asked.

Greg chuckled ruefully. "She can handle a gun as well as you. Later, she was nice and pleasant enough. I liked her, for that matter."

"She's very pretty," Amanda snapped.

Greg shot a quizzical look at her. "Funny, both of you girls asked nearly the same question about one another."

"Did we? Oh, well, I suppose . . . it's natural."

Greg knew she had intended to say something else but had changed it even as she spoke. The three subsided to silence again, each in his own thoughts. Once, Greg caught Amanda covertly eying him. She instantly moved slightly ahead of the two men and rode with her slender back straight and challenging. They came to the Rocking Chair road and Stern reined to one side.

"I'll leave you here. No point in me going on, since I've been there and don't want to see it again. Corwin, will you be close to your ranch for a week or so?"

"Yes. I have to pick up where Terrall left off."

"Then I'll drop in. By then, you'll figure how you stand after Amanda shows you around."

"Do that, but right now—"

"Wait! Just wait an hour more, that's all."

He touched his fingers to his hat brim, smiled at Amanda and jogged away down the road. Greg watched after him, still trying to judge the man, until Amanda made an impatient sound. "There is still riding to do, Mr. Corwin."

Greg moved into the ranch road with her. They followed it almost to the hills that hid the ranch house itself but then Amanda abruptly cut off the road at an angle to the northeast. Greg followed but she saw his look of surprise.

"We're riding to the Bar Y line. Does that give you a hint?"

They entered a swale that threaded the hills. Beyond, Amanda kept a course to the northeast. They came onto another low line of hills and Amanda said it would not be far now. As Stern had predicted, it was about an hour before Amanda drew rein just within the far mouth of the little canyon they had been following.

"You're a puncher—a rancher. This won't be very nice to see. It was even worse three days ago when we found it. I think you're going to hate Bar Y in a minute or two as much as we do."

She moved ahead. Greg followed her out into a small valley that swept northward to a far line of hills beyond the straight glittering barbed-wire fence. So those far hills, he knew, were on Bar Y range. Then he saw, this side of the fence, at least a score of forms lying on the grounds.

At first he could not make them out and looked at Amanda. Her face had turned pale and she spoke between clenched teeth. "We'll get closer."

A few yards farther on, he caught a faint scent of death, a vestige of what must have been overpowering a few days ago. He began to understand. He involuntarily drew rein and Amanda pulled silently in beside him, closely watching. Greg forgot her and, forced by a horrible, stunned fascination, moved slowly forward, eyes held on the shapes before him.

He finally drew rein again and sat like a man of stone, gaze slowly moving over the scattered forms. He looked on dead cattle—on shreds of hide torn from the white arches of great ribs, the bones of legs and haunches exposed by the scavengers of the area. There was little left of the beasts. His jaw tightened and his tawny eyes hardened as he turned to Amanda.

She looked straight ahead, lovely face nearly bloodless. Her voice came in a tight half-whisper from lips that had thinned like a wound.

"Over twenty head. Prime Rocking Chair beef. Just the week before we brought salt cakes for the cattle we knew grazed this part of our range. Then . . ."

"How? Poison?"

"Rifle bullets. What with the hills and distance, I didn't hear the shots at the house. The crew worked our range west and south. But buzzards—and wolves at night, or coyotes and foxes. Ants—maybe all the time. More buzzards, so many I could see them against the sky from the house. Not a dot or two, like you generally see them, but so many they looked like a turning black wheel now and then."

She took a deep breath, breasts rounding fully beneath her loose blouse. "I wheeled Dad to the window and he guessed what it might be. I rode up here and found 'em. They were only half—it was awful!"

She tightly closed her eyes a second and then her voice grew stronger. "I rode straight to where the crew was working. We came back but . . . what could anyone do then? Over twenty head! Know how much loss that is?"

Greg almost shuddered, nodded. "And you think Bar Y did it?"

Her expression suddenly exploded into fury and her eyes blazed at him. But she checked hot words, lifted the reins and said, "Come with me."

She picked her way between the dead animals, continued on a distance and stopped. She pointed to the ground and then her arm swept northward to the fence. "We found sign here—still a bit of it left, see?—of riders coming from beyond the fence. They rounded up our beef. Understand?—

73

rounded up—and then . . . this. There was sign leading north again. I'll show you something else."

She spurred on toward the distant fence. A moment later, Greg raced after her. He came abreast and they rode swiftly to the fence, followed it several yards and Amanda pointed to a whole section of new wire. She swung out of the saddle and Greg dismounted. She pointed to older wire beyond the next post and then touched the four strands of new beside her.

"This whole section had been cut and was down and the trail led directly into our range then back over into Bar Y."

As Greg studied the fence, she said, "I ordered this new wire strung. It sounds crazy to repair Bar Y's own fence, doesn't it? But Yates and Edwards would like nothing better than Rocking Chair beef drifting onto their range. After the killing here, what would they do then?"

Greg turned from the fence to look at the distant dead cattle. Amanda, in her anger and the eagerness of her argument, now stood close beside him. He became too much aware of her but she apparently didn't notice. She insisted, "Can you trust the word of an outfit that would do this to your neighbor? Whatever you were told or promised means nothing. You can bet on it."

"Maybe. But until then, I have to keep my word, don't I?"

"But you see this!"

"I see it," he nodded grimly, "and I'd sure like to get hold of the sneak riders that did it."

"Then—"

"Tracks, cut fence—but did you see the riders?"

"Of course not! They didn't wait around to get caught."

"Then how do you know it was Bar Y? Did they cut their own fence and leave clear sign so you'd know who'd done it? Neither Edwards nor Yates looked like fools to me. Did you call in the sheriff?"

"Yes—and he said there was no proof against Bar Y. You

74

and he talk alike." She moved even closer, her eyes sparking angrily. "And Bar Y *would* let us know! It's a clear warning. Sell out or else."

He looked at the replaced wire again and suddenly asked, "What do you know about a burned out Bar Y line shack just beyond my boundary?"

"Nothing! When did it happen?"

"About the time, or just before, this." He indicated the distant still forms. "Bart Yates tried to accuse me. Then he said wire was cut down this way and a trail led to the burned shack. Bar Y fence was cut but nobody rode over my range. Maybe some of your friends might have done it?"

"No! No, I would have heard. But maybe Hobe Terrall?"

"Not Hobe. Cal would've told me. Besides, from what I've learned about him, Hobe was too scared. He planned to sell out to Bar Y before I came along—like a fool, wandering dogie!"

"I don't know then. I honestly don't. I doubt if the others would have made a move like that without telling me. No, none of us."

She pointed back toward the dead cattle. "Main thing is, Bar Y did that. All of us—and that means you—have to band together to fight Bar Y. We can't do it alone, one at a time. That's the way Bar Y is picking us off. But banded together . . ."

She grasped his hand and almost pressed against him. Her eyes, snapping with the fervor of her argument a second before, suddenly became soft. Greg looked into deep brown pools that held him enchanted. Her lips, so close, subtly moved as though to shape a secret that she could only tell to him. Her gusty breathing lifted her breasts and it seemed the cloth of her blouse touched him. Her fingers pressed down on his hand and he felt as though he held his breath. She was no longer the partial tomboy in levi and boots, but a woman full molded. He had to check the powerful impulse to bend his head and kiss her as he swept her in.

Her voice became low, breathless. "We need you—every one of us, Greg. That's true. You know it. Hobe Terrall didn't have the nerve to face Bar Y. You guessed that. But you—I know *you* do. Throw in with us before Bar Y swallows us —and Tumbling T will be the first, believe me. Come in with us. With me."

She lifted her face to his, eyes pleading, lips soft. He could feel himself becoming lost, going down before this weapon that only a beautiful woman could use. It would be so easy. And then perhaps she and he— He fought to hold his reason. She neither implied nor promised anything, just instinctively knew the effect she created.

He took a deep breath, spoke with difficulty as a man will who realizes he might be losing something. "The fight started before I came to Sioux Valley. You know why I'm staying out."

"Greg, you can't! Bar Y will just wait for the right time and—"

"I've heard that over and over, and I've thought it over and over. I know I'm gambling but getting in a shooting war is even worse. I told Bar Y to count me out. I'm telling the rest of you. That's final."

Her eyes held his, level, searching and turning slowly cold and then scornful. Her lips curved in an unpleasant smile, the venom of which reached her eyes. She spoke in a low, hissing whisper.

"I've tried to be your friend, Corwin. I've tried to show you facts—like the cattle out there—and you even helped me out of an ambush."

"I'd like to help now but—"

"You're scared as well as a stubborn fool." Her expression momentarily softened and then grew stern again as she won some inner battle. "We've always helped one another here.

76

But don't you count on it now. Just do what you can by yourself when Bar Y comes riding up to take over Tumbling T."

She raced to her horse, sprang into the saddle, wheeled and raced off. Greg watched her circle the cattle and speed away. She grew smaller with distance and finally she became just a speck against low hills, then disappeared.

Greg finally stirred, mounted the bay and spoke a soft word to set the horse in motion. He followed at a slow pace after Amanda, but soon left her trail as he turned his horse toward home.

He came to the main valley road, hardly seeing it. He remembered Amanda's lovely, eager face, her vibrant body so close and could almost feel the warm pressure of her hand on his. His eyes brooded. He wanted to help her and he would if she landed in real trouble. Until then, he must avoid calling trouble down on himself.

Suddenly he recalled that fleeting moment of softness in Amanda's face just before she whirled away from him and rode off. He tried to analyze it but couldn't.

X

When Greg returned to the Tumbling T, Cal met him at the corral and said sourly as Greg dismounted, "Hoskins is still in the parlor and your whiskey stock has sure been dented. He's been at it steady since you left."

"Drunk?"

"Not him! Never saw a man who could hold so much and still get around. No, he just gets more bright-eyed and friendly."

"Then he can talk? . . . You'd better come in and listen, Cal. You'll need to know."

Greg found Hoskins still seated by the little table, a full shot glass in his hand. The level of the bottle had gone down considerably but Hoskins looked up, smiled and spoke without the least slur in his voice.

"Git your riding done, Corwin? 'Tweren't only the bottle kept me here, but I figured you'n me could get acquainted without a lot of fussing back and forth." His look grew sharp. "You saw it?"

"I saw it."

Hoskins handed the bottle to him. "Then maybe some of this will sit good."

Greg hesitated then accepted. He poured a drink and sat down. Cal stood just within the doorway, puzzled. Greg wiped his hands across his lips and told Cal what he had seen.

The old puncher listened and then picked up the bottle himself. "Just thinking of that makes me want a drink."

"You didn't know about it?" Greg asked.

"Not a thing! Bar Y? Sure, that's it."

"What do you know of it, Hoskins?"

"Little more'n you, that's a fact. 'Manda came to my place right after it happened. Wanted me, Sam Ralls and all the little valley ranchers to see it. Sure wasn't nice then, let me tell you."

"It wasn't nice today."

Hoskins emptied his glass. "We held a meeting at Rocking Chair and we figured we'd been given the smoke signal by Bar Y. So it turned into a sort of war palaver—or tried to. Me, I ain't quite ready for that yet. So it ended up we band together, let Yates know it and then wait for the next move. 'Manda said at the meeting we should talk to you, so we rode over today."

"You're sure it's Bar Y's doings?"

Hoskins eyed Greg and then refilled his glass, moved it about in his fingers. "Yes, but maybe not so all-fired certain as the rest of 'em."

"But who else'd do it!" Cal exploded.

"A good question, Hoskins," Greg said. "What's your answer?"

The rancher worked his lips in the rubbery grotesque way of fat men. He scowled, studied his glass, drank. "None. It was deliberate—just mean-evil deliberate. And the sign—"

"I know," Greg cut in. "I saw it, including the cut fence. But Cal and me saw cut fence along our range and a burned out line shack. Yates tried to brand me with it. Trail was all on *his* side, though. Do you figure the beef killers came right

79

on eastward, burned the shack and cut the fence again and then went back the way they came? Yates said that's the way the sign read."

Hoskins lip-chewed on that for a few moments. He looked underbrow at Greg. "If I ride your question out to the end, I land up that someone on our side did both jobs. Is that right?"

"You'd know better'n me. I don't clear Bar Y, understand, but a thing like this would be a good way to bring a range war to a head. Who'd profit one way or another?"

Hoskins' heavy head jerked up and he stared aghast at Greg. Then he blinked rapidly and slowly shook his head. "You reason straight from what you know but it won't hold water."

"Why not?"

"First—and believe me, Corwin!—there ain't a single one of us wants war. It's a risk and a bad one. Some of us would get killed and it would ruin us all. I trust every one of the small ranchers and their hands. I've known 'em. Second, you ask who'd profit? I'd say Bar Y."

"Come on, Hoskins! That—"

"Don't make sense? Chew on it a minute, friend, and let me help you. All of us figure the same jaspers did both jobs, right? . . . Okay, what did Bar Y lose? A line shack and a section of fence—not two, 'cause 'Manda had one section repaired, didn't she?"

Greg nodded and Hoskins grunted forward to the edge of his chair. "But what'd Rocking Chair lose? Enough cattle for Bar Y to build a dozen line shacks and string a heap of wire. So who came out on top? Even more, like 'Manda said and we agreed, Bar Y gave notice that our time's running short."

"A third party, then?"

"There ain't one—except you, unless you throwed in with us while you were riding with 'Manda."

80

"No. I wanted to after what I saw just to get the killers. But there's no law-court proof against Bar Y and I've given 'em my promise. They haven't broken their word so far as I'm concerned and—"

"You stand by yours. I always liked that in a man, even though he might've given it to the wrong person. Like I figure you did. Wish you were with us, we need you, but I understand how you can't be—yet?"

Greg looked up sharply and Hoskins smiled without humor. "That's right—yet. Y'see, I don't trust Bart Yates. Sooner or later, you'll be with us."

Greg sighed, making no other response. He asked gloomily, "When will the shooting start?"

"Hard to say. Depends on Bar Y. Like I said, I'll do what I can to keep me'n my friends from going on a hot-headed war path. That's my word on it. But there does come a time . . ."

His voice faded into silence and the three men looked bleakly at one another. Hoskins refilled his glass, tossed it down and pulled himself to his feet. He swayed a second but then stood firm.

"Nothing more to be said or done until the time comes and then, I reckon, we do what's forced on us. No sense in guessing what that will be. Much obliged for the drinks, Corwin. You come down to my Rafter H sometime."

Greg merely nodded and Hoskins hitched at his trousers. "Well, long ride back. Look to see you soon."

"Maybe."

"Maybe. That's all any of us can say about anything, ain't it?"

Greg and Cal saw Hoskins ride off and then turned back to the house. Cal went into the kitchen and Greg heard the bang of pots and pans. Greg dropped into a chair before his desk in the office and frowned out the window at the slowly fading light. His thoughts moved futilely from fact to fact, from possibility to possibility, from face to face until Amanda's came clear and held in his mind.

He saw her half parted lips so close to his, heard the echo of her eager, appealing voice and then of her scorn. He saw her ride off, contempt in every line of her receding figure. Then there was nothing and he saw the cold, darkening light of the sky through the window. He slapped his hand down on the chair arm and, with a grunt of anger at the whole situation including himself, jumped up and walked to the kitchen.

Cal looked around from the stove. "Settle anything?"

"Nothing."

"Figures. Well, supper's about on, anyhow."

For the next few days, Greg firmly forced the problem out of his mind. He still felt that his attitude of neutrality was the nearest thing to workable and he would waste time worrying until something changed the situation. Cal seemed to read his thoughts and agree, though Greg knew the old man held reservations. They worked through the days as though there was no such thing as Bar Y or Amanda Zane and her friends.

One morning they worked the draws near the Bar Y line, some distance from the burned line shack. They emerged from bushes screening a shallow canyon and saw the wire of the fence ahead of them. At that moment, beyond the fence, half a dozen men emerged from a draw on the Bar Y side.

Cal asked acidly, "Wonder what devilment they're about?"

"Devilment?" Greg echoed. "I'd say they're working their own range."

"Maybe, but knowing—"

"Leave it alone, Cal. Everyone in Sioux Valley is suspicious of everyone else. That's half the trouble."

Cal did not reply but rode frowning with Greg out onto

82

the open grass slope down from the canyon. Beyond the fence, the riders suddenly halted in a bunch, obviously watching. Greg rode unconcernedly on, paralleling the wire.

"Hey! Corwin!"

The voice shouted across the distance and Greg drew rein. A rider had left the bunch and Greg instantly recognized Bart Yates' heavy body. Greg turned to the fence to meet the man. Cal, close beside him, said dryly, "Just minding their business? How come this? Anyhow, watch him."

Greg reined in as Bart Yates came up to his side of the fence and both men eyed one another over the wire. Yates shot a single, contemptuous and dismissing glance at Cal and then his black eyes centered on Greg.

"Seems like you can't keep far away from our fence, Corwin."

Beyond Yates, the riders drifted forward. Greg caught the movement as he answered, "I could say the same."

"Lately, folks have a habit of cutting our wire. You still don't know nothing about it?"

"Not much. I asked around."

"Oh, did you now! I suppose all your friends are just little white woolly lambs."

"Maybe not, but none of them are fence cutters or shack burners."

"Just happened all by itself, huh? Reckon we didn't think of Indian spooks or something? So you asked around. I take it that means you're getting friendly over the Valley. You promised Vale—"

"I'd not take sides. I haven't. Does that keep me from meeting folks?"

"Reckon not, but one thing leads to another. I didn't put much stock in your word at the house the other day. I don't now. You'll turn sidewinder if you get the chance."

Greg sensed Cal's angry start but Greg only smiled

83

tightly. "I've heard a man reads in others only what he knows is in himself. Better wait and see, Yates."

The man's dark face suffused as his nostrils flared to a deep breath. Now his men formed a half moon behind him. "Corwin, you puff up into a bigger hoptoad every minute. Someday you're going to bust yourself sure. Or someone'll do it for you."

"I'm puffing on my own range and by myself. Ain't likely someone else will bust me unless he goes to a mighty lot of trouble. Hear a man gets warts if he fools around with hoptoads too much."

Yates glared and then lifted the reins. "Still puffing! Well, have your fun while you can."

He started to rein around but Greg said, "I saw dead beef over on Rocking Chair, near your line fence. They'd been shot. Since your fence was cut and the trail—"

Yates whipped around. "The sheriff cleared us of that."

"So I heard. But what do you *know* about it?"

Yates leaned his weight on his hands resting on the saddle horn and his expression grew darkly wicked. "Not a thing. Tell that to your friends. And tell 'em Bar Y's getting tired of 'em, too. I wouldn't give a damn if all of you lost every head of stock you're running."

"Sounds like a threat, but I'll tell 'em."

"Do that. Compliments of Bar Y."

He wheeled about and rode off. His men eyed Greg and Cal as they turned to follow. Cal broke the long silence when the cavalcade at last disappeared. "Yates kept spurring. Did he want a fight?"

"I don't know. Might be just his nature. Or maybe he changed his mind."

Cal swiped his face with a crumpled bandanna. "Let's get back to work."

At the end of the week, Greg drove the buckboard into Redman for supplies, Cal trotting his gray horse alongside.

84

Greg partially circled the square until he found an empty hitchrack and pulled in. Cal tied the gray and the two men walked to the general store.

It was filled with punchers and townspeople. They curiously eyed Greg but none spoke. Greg frowned at this lack of the usual range courtesy. Cal explained in a low voice as they examined harness at the back of the store.

"Word's spread about you. Those are Anchor and Rocking Chair people and some from the south of the valley. They've heard you ain't taking sides—or maybe that you've thrown in with Bar Y."

The people in the store moved slowly about the aisles, buying supplies, exchanging comments. Now and then Greg caught searching, weighing eyes on him but they would slide away when they met his. There was no real hostility, only reserve and withdrawal. He would not be admitted to their company until they were sure of him.

Greg and Cal spent a long time in the store, for there was much to buy. They finally loaded the buckboard, roped the cargo down and their mission was over. Greg said, "Stand you drinks, Cal, if you feel dried out."

"That I do and thanks." The old man frowned back at the store. "But I'd like to know more of what's going on. They could at least pass a civil word, no matter what they've heard about you. Something's happening and we've been cut out."

"No reason why they should tell us."

"But every reason we should know. Man's a fool to ride blind even if he ain't taking a hand." Cal swung around. "Might be I'd learn something if I was alone. I'll hit a couple of the punchers' saloons and you go to the Rancher's Rest. See you around in an hour or so."

They parted, Cal loafing along the planked sidewalk toward a saloon down the street. Greg walked the short distance to the Rancher's Rest and entered.

This time, every table had one or more occupants. Greg, stopping just within the door, instantly saw Bart Yates seated alone at a far table. Their eyes met across the room, locked for a tense second and then Yates deliberately shifted about so his broad back spoke a flat rejection.

Greg became aware that men studied him with noncommittal reserve. His jaw faintly tightened but he'd not turn tail on this rejection. He walked to the bar, where Lafferty gave him a nod and a faint smile. Greg started to order when a hand dropped lightly on his shoulder.

He turned to face Unger's smile. "Glad to see you again, Corwin."

"It's good someone is. Have a drink?"

"Thanks—at my table." He turned before Greg could reply and led the way to a place not far from Bart Yates, who sourly watched them. Greg sat down as Unger poured a drink and pushed it to him. "How's your deal with Bar Y working out?"

"All right, I reckon."

"You mean to say there's no open trouble yet. Word goes around you're backing Bar Y."

"A lie."

"Maybe—but they believe it. They tell me what they think."

"Let them think it, then."

Unger looked about to make sure he would not be overheard. "Do you know that Amanda Zane has finally had her way? Every ranch but you has thrown in to block Bar Y—the solid front she always wanted."

"She asked me. I refused."

"That's why there are hard feelings against you. You'll be trapped between two fires."

"I'll face that when it comes."

Unger's voice lowered grimly. "Give it a month, then. No more. Things have built up to the point where one little

86

thing could blow Sioux Valley wide open. Why, even you might be the spark."

"Me!"

"They all suspect you, both sides. You could unknowingly make a false move. That would do it. You're like a neutral country between enemy nations, a battleground and nothing you could do about it."

"You're telling me I can't win either way."

"Except my offer still stands."

"No, thanks. I figure to come out even, at least."

"You won't." Unger emptied his glass and stood up. "Think it over and figure every angle. I have. You'll come out a little ahead with my offer."

"You mean less of a loss."

"If that's the way you see it. But things won't be the same—say, in ten days. By then, you can keep Tumbling T for what it's worth. Be glad to see you anytime between now and then. Afterwards . . . don't bother."

He smiled and walked away. Greg watched him leave the saloon. Then Greg covertly looked around at the men in the room. He felt the wall between him and them. He looked toward Yates, studying the man's harsh profile. There was no mercy or understanding in him, Greg knew. Only Vale Edwards held him in leash and Unger had just said the leash could easily snap.

Hal Stern suddenly loomed across the table. "I'd like to talk to you, Corwin."

"Sit down."

Stern eased into a chair. "I'll not waste time. Amanda told me we can't count on you. Maybe, like my friends, I should let you alone. But in a way that'd be a mistake."

"Why?"

"Say I'm taking a last chance, figuring you don't know your spread will catch the first bit of hell, either way. Anyhow, you could change your mind and we'd welcome you. In a reasonable length of time."

"Like a week or ten days?"

Hal Stern gave him a puzzled look. "Are you setting your own time limit? All right, if you want it that way."

"I want it no way."

"But your own." Stern pulled himself out of the chair. "But that ain't possible . . . not at all. If you change your mind, let me or Amanda know—anyone of us, for that matter."

"I will, if—and it's a big if."

Stern's eyes glinted a second before he turned away, threaded the tables to the door. Greg settled into his chair and gazed morosely at his whiskey. Unger gave him a week, Stern hinted time ran out and Cal Weber sensed that something moved under the surface. All of a pattern?

Greg looked at the big clock over the bar but settled himself to give Cal time to find out what he could. Greg toyed with his drink, his mind creating pictures of what might be —of Bar Y riders war-bound across his range, of counterraids by the small ranchers. Would both strike at him because he would not take sides?

For the first time, Greg had serious doubts about his stand. It took at least two to be neutral; the man who wanted to stay clear and those who would let him. He suppressed a faint shiver, tossed down his drink and hurried outside.

He studied the square, hoping to see Cal, then walked toward the nearest of the town's lesser saloons. He passed his loaded and lashed buckboard before the general store. Diana Edwards emerged and stopped short when she saw him. She exclaimed softly, "Why, Mr. Corwin! It's good to see you again."

"Thanks, ma'am. A pleasure."

"Really?"

88

"Really." He swept off his hat and stood before her, trying to veil his look that swept over her figure. Today, she wore a light blue dress that in some strange way was even more revealing than the levis and blouse he last remembered. A wide-brimmed straw hat, flower trimmed, shaded her face but he caught the full impact of her knowing eyes.

"How have you been?" she asked.

"All right. Busy."

She smiled. "And no trouble from the bad Bar Y outfit?"

"None at all." He grinned in return. "And hope to have none."

"You won't, Mr. Corwin. I had hoped you'd ride over to pay a friendly call. Dad has spoken about you now and then."

"Well . . . a lot to do right now, you understand." Her eyes said she did but that was no excuse. He felt his neck growing red as he floundered. "Been thinking about it but . . . just couldn't get away. When I can . . ."

She did not lessen the impact of eyes and smile, made a slight movement that made him too much aware of her figure. She extended her hand. "That's a promise, Mr. Corwin. You'll be welcome."

He enveloped her hand in his, swallowed hard, realized she tried to release her fingers. He dropped her hand, stepped aside and, with a final smile, she flowed away down the walk. He stood watching, hat in hand, and then realized he must look like a dolt. He squashed his hat on his head, turned on his heel and strode away.

He found Cal at the second saloon and slid into a chair at the old man's table. Cal said in a low, grim voice, "Rocking Chair—that means Amanda Zane—finally has her way. All but you against Bar Y and they're just waiting for Yates to make a wrong move."

"We've known that, but does Yates?"

"Nothing much happens he don't know."

"Then he'll make a move. If he doesn't, the others will figure he's bluffed."

"And they'll make the move," Cal finished. "Like two hackling dogs circling one another, looking for a throat slash."

Greg glanced at the old man's empty glass. "Ready to head home?"

"Speaking of being ready, how about you in this business?"

"Let's get yonderly."

Greg arose and Cal pulled himself up. They went out on the porch and started to the steps. Suddenly Bart Yates loomed up before Greg, blocking his way. Greg heard Cal's indrawn hiss and became aware that half a dozen hard-eyed men had formed a rough half moon around him, Yates standing a step ahead of the others.

"When I first met you, Corwin, I gave you a warning. But I saw you stop her when she came out of the store. Do you think I work my jaws just to blow up a wind?"

"You're wrong, Yates. I—"

Yates' fist slammed without warning into Greg's stomach. It doubled him forward and a fist cracked off his jaw, straightening him and flinging him back against the saloon wall with a bone-thudding crash.

XI

Stunned, Greg bounced off the wall toward Yates, who waited with a wide grin, his right fist ready to slam home again. Greg half sensed danger and his arms weakly lifted, too slowly. Yates had only to drive home the finishing blow.

Cal Weber suddenly moved in, swinging for the big fore-man's head. Yates whipped around, ducking, and Cal's fist whistled harmlessly through air. Yates caught him in a talon grip, whirled him about and into the arms of one of his men. The puncher's fist, driven into his chest, sent Cal stumbling backward, arms wildly flailing.

In these few seconds, Greg managed to find his balance. Yates wheeled back around to finish the job and Greg caught a split-second flick of surprise in the narrowed eyes as he threw a punch at Yates' jaw.

Yates jerked his head aside just enough that Greg's knuckles scraped along his jaw. But the force of the blow made Yates give a half step. Greg bored in, shifting to the man's stomach just above the belt buckle. His fist slammed home.

There was only firm muscle. Yates grunted, however, and

91

gave another step. Now both men stood at the edge of the porch. Yates slid away, sensing the drop at his boot heels. He made a low feint, crossed, and his blow landed beside Greg's ear, making his head ring and blinding him.

Greg dimly heard shouts from the street below and the batwings behind him. Cal gave a cracked screech but Greg cut out everything but the big body and dark face bearing down on him. He blocked a punch to the ribs. He slammed his fist into hard muscled stomach again and Yates stepped to the left. Greg saw the blow coming toward his chin like a pile driver. He threw elbow and forearm in the way, saw an opening and tried for the man's mouth.

Greg felt lips smash against his knuckles and the ripping cut of teeth. Yates' head snapped back. Greg moved in as the man retreated along the edge of the porch. Greg threw blows left and right, trying for chin or body, but Yates blocked them, face pain twisted, blood trickling from nose and cut lips.

Greg aimed for the stomach again before Yates could drop his guard. Greg's fist slammed home and this time Yates' breath whooshed out and he doubled forward. Greg's left moved up like a cracking whip and he felt the solid smack of the blow. Yates swayed an instant, completely exposed. Greg lunged in to end the battle.

A boot struck between his legs and he stumbled as someone caromed into him, throwing him aside and away from Yates. One of the Bar Y men spun away as Greg turned to meet the new assault. He glimpsed a stubbled face with squint eyes and a crooked, broken nose. It flicked through his mind he had seen that face before, but he sensed a rush behind him and wheeled to meet Yates' attack. As they collided in a thunder of stomping boots on the wooden floor, Yates' knee came up in a vicious blow. Fiery pain flooded from groin to brain, racking Greg and wiping away all sight and sound. He knew only torture but vaguely sensed his arms had dropped, his body bent.

Something struck him in the jaw. He had a brief sensation of falling before all consciousness snapped out.

Somewhere in a peculiar melange of black space and foggy time, a small dot of pain faintly registered. It exploded into stabbing thrusts of torturing hot iron as Greg became aware of body immersed in agony he could not escape. He clawed his way toward consciousness.

He became aware of light coming in sword-edge slits and realized his eyes had partially opened. Then pain swept in and he swung off into darkness with it. It was better in the darkness but the dull monster lurked somewhere ready to pounce. He had a sensation of something sweet and cloying choking off his breath. He fought it an eternity, it seemed, but could not win. The darkness held a peculiar green tinge and then even the darkness was gone.

He opened his eyes with the feeling that unrealized days and days had swept by. Pain was now a constant, boring pressure in his lower abdomen and, strangely, his face. He saw a lamp, burning low, on a strange table. He saw a far wall, a desk and a cabinet in half shadows, bottles on shelves behind the glass doors reflecting slivers of light.

A shadow loomed near and Cal Weber looked worriedly down at Greg. His wrinkled face went slack with relief. "You've come around!"

Greg's dull brain digested the words. His voice sounded distant, strange and muffled. "How long?"

"It's past midnight."

The statement sunk in. Greg's eyes widened and he started up. He could not check his sharp yelp and catch of sobbing breath, as he dropped back again. He bit at lips and clutched his abdomen. As though his fingers had literally checked the pain, it slowly receded and he could breathe in sharp gulps that finally eased off.

"What happened? Yates?"

Cal asked, "You'll be all right? The doctor's right outside. This is his office."

"How'd I get here?"

"Carried. You were in no condition to walk. Yates kneed you good. Thought for a time he'd killed you. But ne'er mind that. How you feel?"

Greg took a slow, cautious, testing breath. "I don't need the doctor. Not now, anyhow. Yates?"

Cal pulled a chair up beside the bed and sat down. "First, that jasper tripped you and then Yates come in. He used his knee. A minute later, you were on the floor and rolled off the porch. Me'n another brought you here. Doc says you'll be all right in a few days."

Greg thought of turning but a twinge as he barely moved changed his mind. "I keep asking about Yates."

"He don't look very pretty, that's a fact. He and his crew walked off after he downed you. He told me you'd get more of the same if you bothered Diana Edwards again. He said he meant anywhere and anytime."

Greg's angry grimace made his face ache and he became aware of sore muscles all over his body below the main, continuing pain. "There'll be another meeting sometime. This time, I'll watch his knee."

"And any other crooked move! and his crew!" Cal snapped. "Wasn't for that knothead tripping you—"

"Maybe. Yates is hard to stop, like a bull."

Cal rubbed his jaw with long, thoughtful strokes of his crooked fingers. Greg remembered. "What'd they do to you?"

"Pushed me around, kept me from helping. Took more'n one of 'em to do it, though!"

Greg made a flick of a smile and became aware of the taste in his mouth, a faint cloying scent about his nose. "What'd the doctor do?"

94

"Looked you over while two of us held you down. You pain-wiggled like a snake, I swear! Then he used chloroform to put you to sleep. After that, he could look you over and said no real damage. You just ain't gonna want to move around much."

Cal walked to the door and called. Doc Robbins entered, a wiry, bronzed little man with a great shock of iron gray hair. He asked questions that Greg answered with a nod or a grunt. Robbins held a palm on Greg's forehead, looked satisfied. "You'll make it. Can you sleep? I could knock you out again?"

"No, I'll stick with it the way it is."

"Just bite down. It might come in waves for a time. It'll take time to walk good and to ride. Don't rush it."

"When can I go home?"

"Come morning, we'll see if you can ride the buckboard."

Greg dismissed Cal, who protested but reluctantly left. The lamp burned low through the long, dark hours of the night. There were periods, seemingly eternal, when Greg wished he'd accepted another sniff of the chloroform. But the pain always subsided to a harsh, continuing ache.

Now and then Greg slipped into light, half feverish naps. He gritted teeth and stared dully at the medicine cabinet, the desk and the low lamp flame. He thought of Yates with a growing anger bordering on hate. The man could have crippled him for life. Gradually Greg realized that Yates might cripple another unless he had a hard lesson he could understand.

So be it! Yates would get fists again and he'd know why, if Greg had to ride to Bar Y itself.

His thoughts fastened on Diana Edwards, skipped on to her father and then the whole Sioux Valley situation. What effect would the fight have? Unger had said that Greg himself could tip the scales to open war. Greg mentally shook his head. Not this—it was personal, over a girl and all because of Yates' jealousy. No, not the whole valley's fight—Greg Corwin's.

He drifted into sleep just before dawn. When he awakened, the sun was up and an Indian squaw came bearing a tray of breakfast and coffee. The odor of the food was like a tonic. He started up but dropped back with an involuntary cry.

The Indian woman thudded phlegmatically across the room in a flat footed walk. She placed the tray on the table, pulled it and chair to the bed, waited until Greg stopped twisting. "Boss-Doc say you no good eat yourself. Me feedum."

"I'll . . ." wrenched from Greg's breath, ". . . I'll take care of my eating."

"No good. Boss-Doc say feedum. Me feed. You not move. Hurtum." She spooned up mush and thrust the instrument at Greg as she would a stick. He could take the mush on his face or in his mouth. His lips snapped open. She grunted, "Good!"

It was—and the second and third spoonful. He felt futile anger but he submitted and toward the end, after deep-buttered toast, fried eggs and aromatic coffee, enjoyed it in a perverse way.

Doc Robbins appeared as the process ended. He watched, grinning, from the foot of the bed and then signalled the Indian away. She thudded out with tray and empty dishes and Doc took her seat.

"I have a call ten miles out of town. When I get back, we'll see how you can move. By the way, how do you like Morning Dove? Delicate wench, isn't she?"

"Like an elephant!"

"You miss the interior quality. If you can be moved, would you prefer home or the town's hotel? The hotel's not bad, by the way."

"Home."

96

"We'll see. Rest until I get back."

He started to the door. Greg called, "Doc! How's Yates?"

Doc's voice grew cold. "I didn't treat him. Doubt if I would now, unless really serious. He was battered. You left your mark, if that helps."

"A little, Doc, just a little."

That afternoon, with grunts, stabs of pain and the help of Cal, Greg managed to get into the buckboard that Cal had brought around. Greg stretched out amid sacks and bundles. Cal drove as carefully as he could but, even so, Greg saw the ranch house through a haze of pain, eased down into his bed with a relieved sigh, wondering how long he'd be crippled up.

Several days passed and, gradually, Greg managed to move about the house, fretful that he couldn't help Cal with the ranch work. But the old man brushed Greg's irritable protests aside.

During this time, Greg thought long and hard about Bart Yates, Bar Y and the Sioux Valley trouble. He had been right in his first assessment of the fight. Diana Edwards unwittingly had caused it, so this had been two men fighting, not two factions. Greg still felt fiery anger about the puncher tripping him and the knee in the groin. That would have to be evened up and Greg intended to. But, and Greg gave a long period of brooding thought on it, this did not mean Vale Edwards was implicated. Greg's promise of neutrality would still hold.

At last, Greg was able to mount the bay, ride it for short periods that he extended over the succeeding days until he could ride with a minimum of discomfort. He told Cal one morning when the old man came in from the barn, "I can handle my share now. And it's about time!"

"Don't push it," Cal warned as they turned to the house from the barn.

"I haven't. I feel fine. Like new."

They entered the kitchen and Greg poured coffee as Cal wearily dropped onto a chair by the table. He underbrowed his thanks to Greg, sipped gratefully at the hot brew and then eased back. "Can't say I don't need your help. But make sure."

Greg dropped on the chair across the table with his own mug of coffee. "I am. How does it look today?"

"We'd better throw out some salt cakes, I figure. Beef's fattening up and the calves coming along. Might have a good year if they just keep the lid on the valley."

"Let's hope so. Nothing's happened."

"Except to you."

"That's not the valley. I'll take care of it myself."

Cal worked at his coffee, lowered the mug. "Speaking of the devil, I was up at Bar Y fence and saw—"

"Bart Yates?"

"Nope, that squint-eyed jasper that tripped you in the fight."

Greg searched back for an elusive memory. "That one . . . I've seen him before . . . before the fight, that is."

"He's one of the hardcase bunch Yates brought in from outside when he started ramrodding Bar Y. Ain't been here long."

"Saw him somewhere else, then, do you reckon?"

"Drifting gunslinger, that one. Might be you did."

"All right, maybe . . . but let it go."

Cal suddenly peered out the window. "Company of some kind coming."

Greg bent to the window. He could see just a small bit of the distant road before it curved to the house and the structure cut it off. Greg glimpsed two riders but sensed, from the roiling dust cloud, that more had moved beyond his view. Then the two disappeared. "How many? Who?"

"Half a dozen at least. One I swear is Hoskins and one 'Manda Zane."

98

"Another argument!"

"Maybe. Looked more like real trouble."

Greg walked down the hallway, Cal just behind him. He stepped out on the porch and waited at its edge as the cavalcade approached. They were still some distance away but he confirmed Hoskins and Amanda, recognized Hal Stern. The four other men were strangers.

Amanda, slightly ahead of the rest, pulled in a few yards out and the others bunched behind her. Greg called, "Light and rest your saddles."

"Not much time. We're riding to Redman for the sheriff."

"That'll do a lot of good!" Hal Stern burst out.

Greg searched their grim faces. "More trouble, I see. What this time?"

"Murder! Tell him, Hal."

Stern moved forward. "I found Sam Ralls. He had two forty-four slugs in his back. Not five minutes before, I had come on a Bar Y hand. He shied off before I was in fair shouting distance and bee-lined for home range."

"He did it?" Greg demanded.

"Who else! Sam had just time to say 'Bar Y' and then he was gone. I lost the best boss I ever had and, believe me, I'm making Bart Yates and that whole damn' crew pay for it!"

"We all are," Amanda cut in.

"But—the sheriff?" Greg asked.

"We're holding to the law as long as we can. We're asking him to arrest Bart Yates and the rider Hal saw—the whole crew over there if we have to. Moyers might be Bar Y's catspaw but we'll still give him a chance to act on the evidence."

"If he doesn't?"

She leaned forward. "You're thinking like we are, Corwin. He won't. So we'll act—and it's been too long coming."

99

Hoskins, just beyond Stern, protested uneasily. "Now, 'Manda, don't make your mind up afore—"

"It's done!" Amanda twisted savagely about in her saddle to face the fat rancher. "Sam was back-shot. Murdered! Can you argue that down?"

She waited, a poised and lovely fury, but Hoskins could only shake his head reluctantly. Amanda settled to her saddle again, facing Greg. "You have some marks Bart Yates left on your face, Corwin. The whole Valley knows what happened. After that, we expected you to come riding to help us. Then we'd heard he'd laid you up. Is that so?"

"Nothing permanent. You can see that."

"Then you've got no excuse to hold back. Sam was cut down without a chance by the same man who marked you."

Greg's bleak tawny eyes studied the hard, expectant faces before him. His gaze returned to Amanda and he wondered what jeering fate kept coming between them. He rubbed the palms of his hands along his trouser legs.

"No excuse. But no reason, either." He saw the shock in her and hurried on. "Get the sheriff. I'll ride with a posse after anyone the lawman names. If Bar Y is behind this murder and it can be proved—"

"Nothing's ever been proved against them! You know that by now."

"Yes, I've heard. When the sheriff names the killer, I'll ride with you, or anyone, as a sworn posseman. Until then . . . no."

He heard the concerted gasp. Stern made an angry move, checked himself. Amanda settled back in her saddle and eyed him as she would a repulsive animal. She lifted the reins and spoke calmly, but her voice a knife that peeled off skin.

"Corwin, I don't believe you—all those high sounding words you pull up from somewhere! Your promise! Proof! —all that!"

"I can't help what—"

"I believe it's more than that." Her lips curled. "You fought over Diana Edwards. The whole Valley knows it. A street brawl over a woman!"

"Now just a minute!"

"Minute—hell! It's true. And that red-headed flirt keeps you from doing what you should right now . . . Well, Mr. Corwin, if you're that far gone, you're welcome to her. She's what you deserve."

She spurred and whipped her horse around so swiftly the cavalcade became tangled for thrashing moments. Then she broke free, racing away. The men wheeled about to follow after her. Stern glared at Greg, spat toward him before he rolled spurs and thundered after the rest.

Greg stood motionless, face drained. Then, sensing Cal, blood rushed up his neck and into his face. The speeding figures grew smaller down the road, the dust roiling high behind hoofs whose thunder slowly faded. Greg didn't move.

Cal cleared his throat. "If 'Manda's right, I wonder why I work for you."

Greg did not turn about. "What will that bunch do now?"

"They'll get the sheriff, take him to Anchor. After that, depends on what Moyers does. They'll ride to Bar Y in any case."

"As posse or vigilantes—it won't matter, will it?"

"Damn it, Greg!"

"Yes, damn it—and all Sioux Valley! And my coming here, for that matter."

He whipped about. Cal moved to the door, turned and looked coldly at Greg. "No matter what's on your mind, Greg—redhead or something else—you could at least help your neighbors bring justice to sneak killers."

"That would be Bar Y? Just no point in arguing, looking, or asking anything?"

"Who else?"

Greg brushed by Cal into the house. When he came out of his bedroom, he had his gunbelt about his waist and carried his rifle.

Cal pulled up short. "By God, you're going to ride after all!"

Greg didn't bother to answer as he hurried through the kitchen and out to the corral.

XII

Greg ordered Cal to stay around the house then wheeled the bay about and set spurs. The first lunging strides jolted him but he felt slightly better when he turned down the main road toward Redman. Somewhere far ahead Amanda and the blood-hungry ranchers rode for a lawman they believed would do nothing. They might be right, Greg thought. In that case, someone has to keep the factions apart until a murderer could be found.

He came to the sign pointing to Bar Y and drew rein. He studied the ground, looking closely to distinguish old trail from new. He moved the horse about and then finally straightened. So far as he could determine, Amanda Zane had led her vengeance riders directly to Redman instead of turning off.

He gave a small sigh of relief. But—he looked along the Bar Y road to where it turned into the low defile between the hills—he now faced other and quite immediate worries. After his fight with Yates, what reception could he expect now?

He pulled the rifle from its scabbard, made sure a shell

nested in the chamber. He eased the rifle back into the scabbard to avoid the slightest bind of leather against the weapon. He loosened his Colt by working it in the holster several times. He momentarily felt the bleakness of the lone wolf but shrugged it off as something about which he could do very little. With an outward confidence that he couldn't quite believe himself, he urged the bay into the Bar Y road. He sharply eyed the slopes and trees, aware that Yates or one of his men might already have spotted him and now waited, concealed, with ready rifle or Colt.

He suppressed a faint shiver with a grim set of his jaw. He rode into the pass and only then slowed his speed. His right hand hung at his side, fingers constantly brushing holster leather and smooth, walnut pistol grip. His eyes moved constantly from side to side and ahead.

He approached the far end of the pass and came to the half concealed draw where Diana Edwards had surprised him. He moved slowly, aware that a more deadly watcher might wait there. But nothing happened. All his senses, tightly extended and aware, suddenly flashed an intuitive knowledge that he rode alone down the pass.

There was no logic to it but he instinctively responded, tight shoulder and back muscles easing off, right arm losing its explosive stiffness. His eyes made one final sweep of the canyon slopes and then concentrated on the opening ahead.

He came to the mouth of the canyon. He looked down the slope, gaze following the cinnamon colored road to the valley, across it to the distant grouping of structures that marked Bar Y. He saw no riders and could detect no movement around the buildings. But the distance could be tricky and he had the feeling that the ranch knew of his presence and waited for him to ride into a trap.

He started the bay down the slope at an easy walk. Within the first hundred yards anyone at the distant ranch could see him. There was no cover. He could only hope that he'd get close enough to parley before riders came out to meet him.

Now he could see the ranch house, barns and the whole complex in more detail. Nothing moved and he suddenly wondered if Bar Y, like Amanda Zane, had taken to the war trail. It made sense if its gunmen had killed Sam Ralls. Greg checked the thought that condemned without proof. Too many had fallen into that trap.

The buildings grew larger under the trees as he lessened distance. He caught movement over toward the corrals and his attention centered there. The cross-hatch of corrals and pens confused his vision but he knew he had at last alarmed the ranch. He touched the rifle, then judged the distance to the ranch house and pulled his hand away. If he had been seen from the outbuildings—and recognized—he had also been identified from the house.

At that moment, half a dozen riders spurred away from the corrals and raced toward him, fanning out into a half circle as they closed the distance. The very shape of the riders bespoke danger. Greg, with a final judging of his distance from the house, drew rein and lifted his hands high above his head. He felt cold sweat over his face but he held the bay steady with pressure of his knees.

The riders checked their speed, sat bolt upright. They could not attack a man waiting with his hands in the air but they could not fully trust the gesture. Yates was not among them. Greg threw a quick look at the house, thinking the foreman might appear on the porch. He saw a lace curtain move erratically at a window, no more.

Now the riders slowly moved in on Greg and he faced the dark, menacing muzzles of at least three guns. He held steady as one man edged ahead of the others. Greg recognized him as one of those who had been on the saloon porch. An instant later, he recognized the man who had blocked his final rush on Yates.

The first man said, "You got a helluva nerve! Yates would like to eat you, alive and kicking."

"Where is he?"

"What's it to you? Just figure you're lucky he's not around right now."

"Then I'll see Vale Edwards."

"Like hell! You'll turn around and ride off."

"When did you become kingpin of the spread?"

The man slightly lifted the Colt in his hand. Greg met his angry eyes and, still holding his arms high, moved the bay forward with a gentle touch of spur. He heard the multiple click of gun hammers dogged back. His face planed and tensed. Greg did not check the slow forward move of the bay. The men looked uncertain, angry, confused. One said to their momentary leader, "How about it, Barney?"

"That's right," Greg said. "How about it? I'm going to the house."

Barney's lips flattened and his gun lifted. Greg sucked in his breath. He had lost the bluff and could not reach his own gun in time nor avoid the bullet.

"Barney!"

The voice came from the house porch. Barney made a spasmodic jerk. For a second, Greg feared reflex action would pull the trigger and he braced to meet the bullet's blow. Then Barney answered in a thick voice, "Yes, Miss Diana?"

"Get back to work. All of you. I can handle this."

"But this jasper—"

"Barney!"

"Yes'm." Then to Greg. "You're just living on the frazzled end of luck, that's all."

He reined about with a signal to the others. They stiffly rode away, looking back at Greg or to the porch where Diana stood, slender, straight and disdainful. Greg felt a sweat-trickle down his back but his throat loosened and he

106

took a quick, deep gulp of air. Then he moved the bay slowly toward the house.

Diana Edwards watched, taking in each single move of animal and rider. When Greg came close, he could see the angry glint in her eyes, an outthrust set of chin and slash of lips. Outraged contempt, he realized. He shifted to dismount but her cutting voice checked him.

"Don't bother to light, Mr. Corwin. You're not welcome here. After what happened in town, I'd think you'd be ashamed to show your face within ten miles of Bar Y."

He flushed. "I don't know what you heard—"

"Plenty!" Her small fist thudded on the porch rail. "What of my reputation, sir! How can I face anyone! My name brought into a saloon fight—and for everyone to hear!"

"Miss Diana, believe me, I had no intention—"

"Oh, it's Bart's fault, is it? I might have expected that. It so happens, he has already told the truth about the affair. I'm grateful someone closed a drunken mouth for my sake."

"You sure got a real story, didn't you?"

"Is there any other?"

"I reckon none that you'd believe. But I didn't come for that."

"I thought it just might be possible you'd at least apologize! If you could in all truth, of course."

"I can say I'm sorry it happened and I'm sorry people gossip over something they know nothing about. But I didn't start either one."

"Oh, indeed—!"

"Look!" he thundered and her mouth hung open in midword. "We're wasting time. You'll not believe me, no matter what I say. That's not important. I have—"

"Not important!" She caught her breath and blazed.

"No! Damn it, no! There's been a murder and Bar Y is blamed. Do I see your father, or do I ride off and let the guns start blasting?"

107

She gulped to bring up the faint question, "Murder?"

"At Anchor, and all the signs pointing right here." He swung out of the saddle and stepped up on the porch. "Ma'am, I see your father one way or another—and right now."

Her anger collapsed. She said in a small voice, "Of course. In that case, Dad's inside."

She cut ahead of him to the door and darted within. Greg moved across the porch, paused at the open door.

"Come in, Corwin. What's this all about?"

He stepped in. Vale Edwards sat in the same chair where Greg had last seen him. But the rigidity of the creased face and the hard eyes lacked welcome. Diana stood beside him, facing Greg and, despite strain and worry, he again felt her impact. He swept off his hat and stood uncertainly. Edwards did not offer the hospitality of a chair.

"Say your piece, sir."

"Sam Ralls has been murdered. Shot in the back. A Bar Y rider was seen nearby just before the Anchor foreman found his boss. He says Sam Ralls claimed that rider shot him."

"It's a lie."

"I hope you can prove it."

"I've just said it's a lie, sir."

"Mr. Edwards, a short while ago half the small ranchers stopped at my place. They told me what had happened and they've made up their minds who did the back-shooting."

Without thinking, Greg sank into a chair. "Maybe I should tell you, since I was last here I've been accused of throwing in on your side, selling out to you, being a traitor and maybe a dozen other things. I've learned that no matter what happens in Sioux Valley, Bar Y is blamed."

"Of course! They hate us!"

"That's certain as daylight, Mr. Edwards. But I keep ask-

108

ing myself, 'Why'. I'm caught in the middle and the noose is getting damn' tight."

"Then join them!"

"No. I made a promise and—"

"Then soiled my daughter's name. I'm glad to see my foreman's marks on your face."

Greg slammed his hat to the floor. "Murder, Mr. Edwards! Murder! A back-shoot and you're blamed. Don't you savvy that! The other argument can wait—and there's two sides to it. But now . . . what about Sam Ralls?"

"What about him? Bar Y had nothing to do with it."

Greg studied the arrogant old face and the proud eyes. He knew that under the facade was reasonableness and a sense of justice. Greg locked his fingers as he sought a means to break through that anger and pride.

"Mr. Edwards, I'm new and maybe for that reason I don't rightly know how things actually came about. Can I tell you what I've learned and heard since I came to Sioux Valley—and since I last saw you? Most you might not like to hear but this is no time to shut eyes and ears to the way things are going."

He threw an underbrow look at Diana. Her attention was fully on him. He saw no trace of her recent anger and contempt, but that most likely would come again, the moment he opened his mouth.

"They tell me there's two Bar Y's—one before and one after Bart Yates came."

"It's the same damn' spread and—"

"Dad, let's listen?"

"Two," Greg repeated. "The one before got along with everyone and no one cared how big it was. But I've heard Yates has changed the whole crew since he came."

"For good reason. Your friends began acting like circling buzzards."

"I'm saying only that I heard a tough-hand crew came on

here and that things began to happen around the valley—
like a man was cut off from every road and had to sell out.
There was a killing 'way to the south and Bar Y bought
the ranch at auction."

"We bought two ranches, Corwin, right enough. One, like
you said, had no way out except over my range. But I never
blocked off a road or a trail."

"Then why'd he sell?"

Diana, a tiny frown wrinkling her forehead, said, "Bart
arranged the deal, Mr. Corwin. The man just wanted to
leave and we couldn't turn down the price. That other deal
—the auction—was fair and legal. The owner was killed—a
range accident. Horse fell on him, we heard."

"You know that for a fact, Mr. Edwards?"

"Certainly. Bart brought the news. By then Bart was re-
porting beef missing every two weeks or so. The sheriff
couldn't find any lead on the rustlers. So Bart and me
figured we had to protect ourselves. He hired tough hands.
I'm old enough to know 'em. Rustling stopped for a time
but started again. We lost line shacks and fences. No
help from the law, either. So Bart brought in a few more
handy men on the crew."

"You say the sheriff didn't help?"

"Not then. But come an election, we had one of our boys
wearing the badge. Just in time, too."

"In time for what?"

"In time to clear us when our neighbors began to make
wild claims, that's what!"

"Is the sheriff your man?—or Yates'?"

Edwards stared, snorted, but didn't look quite so assured.
"Bar Y man. No such thing as his or mine."

Greg let it go by. "Since I've been here, I've found a
burned line shack—yours—and a lot of wire down. Yates
wanted to pin that on me but couldn't."

"From what he told me, you're still not clear."

110

"I am and can prove it. But, something else. I was called over to Rocking Chair to look at a slaughter. Rocking Chair beef rounded up, shot dead and left to rot on the range. Wire cut and the trail came out of and went back into Bar Y. Do you know about that?"

Father and daughter exchanged blank looks then both faced Greg and Edwards shook his head. Greg pressed on. "Now Sam Ralls—and a Bar Y man seen close by."

"This is the first we've heard of it," Diana said and Greg believed her.

He didn't need to ask Vale Edwards—the old man clearly had not known. Greg spoke slowly. "Maybe this time a Bar Y lawman would be like a tangled rope."

"Why, sir? The evidence just can't point to us."

"It does already, so far as I've heard. Like the slaughtered beef—and I saw the sign myself. Like the burned line shack —fence between me and you down but not a single track on my range."

Edwards sat quite still. "If you see it all so much against us, why—considering what happened in town—did you come here?"

"What happened in town is personal between Yates and me. It did *not* concern anything I said or did about Miss Edwards. But all these other things—I'm in the middle. You say the little ranchers are attacking you. They say you're attacking them."

"What do you think?"

"For what it's worth, I think there's too much suspicion and too little proof on either side. What causes it? The way I see it, the little ranchers are lying or you're lying—or there's a third party making profit from the suspicion."

"Who?"

"You talk like Bob Hoskins. He denies it. Maybe I'm wrong but this brings us back to why I've come. Questions about

111

the burning and the dead beef can wait. This one can't. Do you know anything about Sam Ralls' killing?"

"No!"

"Does any of your crew?"

"No!"

"Was there any order given about Ralls? any hint that it'd be a help if he turned up dead?"

Edwards' head jerked up. "You've gone too by-God far! Get out!"

"Mr. Edwards, you're going to have to answer that question, maybe a hundred times. There'll be a lot of people who won't get out when you order them. You know I don't want a range war. So . . . why not start your answering with me?"

Edwards sat stiffly but his body trembled. Diana, her face pale and eyes huge, pressed her fingers into her father's shoulder. He understood the signal. "There was no order nor hint, sir. I am not that kind of man and do not hire that kind of man."

Greg looked beyond him at a clock ticking away on the far wall. He mentally timed the cavalcade into Redman, back to Anchor and then, undoubtedly, to a final war council at Rocking Chair.

"I believe you, sir. Yates is fully in your trust and holds nothing back from you?"

"You hate him," Diana snapped.

"Not near enough to throw suspicion of murder, or cattle killing on him. But you'll get questions thrown at you about him—like was he at the ranch when those cattle were killed? Or when the line shacks burned? Where is he now, for instance?"

Again the exchange of the blank look between father and daughter. Vale answered. "Bart went out early to work the west range. He's not back yet."

Greg scooped up his hat and arose. He looked at the clock.

112

"By now, the sheriff should be at Anchor. I believe you, he's honest. So he's bound to say there's no proof anyone at Bar Y killed Sam Ralls—only Hal Stern's word for what a dying man said. But they'll believe Stern and not an ex-Bar Y lawman."

"So what will they do?" Diana asked.

"They'll go to Rocking Chair, bring all the ranchers together and then they'll come here—rifles ready and ears closed, if you understand me."

Edwards made a rock-hard sound. "We have our own rifles."

"That's the trouble—too many rifles on both sides and too much hard feelings."

"True, on their side. But what can *we* do about it?"

Greg looked from the granite, aged face to the pale beauty and red hair of Diana, her eyes still rounded with the shock of the news. "Let them know Bar Y—you at least —had nothing to do with the murder."

"The sheriff will tell them that."

"They won't believe ex-Bar Y. They will believe you."

Edwards stared. "Do I get your idea—?"

"Let's go to Rocking Chair—you, Miss Diana and me. Just us. They'll not be ready to ride yet. They'll not expect our coming. You can say it straight. It's a long chance, but the only chance of stopping sudden killing."

Edwards' clawed, arthritic hand struck the chair arm. "Be damned if I'll go to them!"

"You'll be damned if you don't—along with some good men fighting for your pride. What about her?"

Greg's head bobbed toward Diana. The three stood tense for long, long moments. Edwards stirred. "Diana, have Tex hitch up the surrey."

113

XIII

———◆———

The old man walked slowly, with help from Diana, to the surrey that Tex and another puncher had brought around to the front of the house. The men watched Edwards grunt, wince and pull himself into the surrey and threw questioning looks at Diana, suspicious glances at Greg. He assisted Diana into the buggy and as she picked up the reins he climbed into the bay's saddle.

Edwards spoke to Tex. "If Bart gets back before I do, tell him to stay hitched—right here. We're going to Rocking Chair."

"Rocking Chair! You need gun siding! I'll get some of the boys."

"You'll do nothing of the kind. If any of you so much as move off this ranch, you're fired. Tell Bart that goes for him."

He dropped back in the seat. Greg spurred ahead until they were out of the yard and onto the road leading into the hills. Then he dropped back to ride alongside the surrey. Diana held the two grays to an easy, steady pace.

She deliberately avoided a direct look at Greg, but this

gave him a chance to study her at his leisure. Beautiful, but Greg sought for something within to match the outer form. He could only judge, of course, from the few times he had seen her, from the way she appeared at this moment. A flirt to a degree and aware of herself as a woman, Greg acknowledged, but that was nothing he could really condemn. All beautiful women he had met had the same instinctive reaction to the eyes of a man. Some used it as Amanda Zane had that day at the fence.

He could tell nothing of her thoughts, for she kept her attention steadily on the road ahead and no slight move of lips or eyes betrayed inward turmoil.

Edwards interrupted his thoughts. "What do you aim to do about Yates?"

Diana looked around and it struck Greg that she waited almost impersonally for his answer. It puzzled him but he had no time to work it out. "Meet him again, somewhere and time when he's not got half the Bar Y crew around him."

Edwards bent with a grimace to peer out and up at Greg. "That happened?"

"Ask Yates."

"He said nothing about it." When Greg didn't answer, Edwards continued, "After what happened to you, I'd think you'd leave him alone."

"It will be different next time. And . . . no lady's name will be pulled into it by anyone."

Diana's chin lifted as she gave full attention to the road again. Edwards sighed. "Can't stop you—or him."

"No. This is between us and has nothing to do with the Valley troubles."

None of them spoke as the road unwound before them, snaking across the valley and around low hills. They came at last to the Tumbling T road and Greg glanced down it toward the hummocks that hid the house from sight. Edwards also followed Greg's gaze, eased back on his cushioned seat. "Have you made changes since Hobe left?"

"Not big ones. You're welcome to see it sometime."

"Thanks, but what would your friends think?"

"No worse than they do right now."

Again silence. At long last they approached Rocking Chair. Diana subtly slowed the pace of the grays. Greg understood, made a small sign of acknowledgment and took full lead. He halted at the road mouth, forcing the surrey to stop.

He pointed north and east. "Over that way—up by your line fence—I saw the dead beef."

Vale's face tightened. "We didn't do it. I'll make the sheriff find out who did."

"Tell that to Amanda and her friends when you see her. It might help."

They threaded the long, wide swale that led through the hills and came out on the little valley where, in almost the exact center, Rocking Chair sat. Greg instantly spotted the line of saddled horses before the house. He spoke over his shoulder. "The pow-wow's on. No Colt or rifle in the surrey, is there?"

"No," Diana answered.

Greg unbuckled his gunbelt and held it swinging at his side as he rode along, the weapon dangling slightly below his right stirrup. He'd not have a chance in the world of reaching the gun in a shoot-out.

He rode straight and steady, hearing the clop of hoofs and whispering roll of wheels behind him. He watched the house. As he came closer, he saw that the conference was being held under a cluster of trees over to the left. At the same moment, he saw a stir among the tree-shadowed group and two or three figures walked out to meet the cavalcade at the ranch gate. One of them, small and slender in a dress, could only be Amanda Zane.

116

Greg did not break pace. He was now close enough to distinguish figures. Amanda Zane moved ahead of Hal Stern and another man Greg did not know. Beyond them, to the left and under the trees, Greg recognized Hoskins' plump figure, a man in a home-made wheel chair and two others, strangers also.

His attention swung back to those at the gate. Amanda stared at the buggy and, for the first time, Greg saw her completely disconcerted. Her dark eyes flashed up at Greg as he drew rein before her and Stern's hand taloned over his holster. Greg said easily, "We're all sitting ducks, if you want to end your war fast."

Amanda's gaze jerked to the surrey and she swallowed, crimsoned. "What do you want?"

"To join your parley."

Stern growled, "You're not invited."

Just at the edge of vision, Greg caught Hoskins' slow approach and it gave him a shade more confidence. He held Amanda with a steady look.

"You're owner, not him." He jerked a thumb back to the surrey. "Here's the people you're accusing of breaking a dozen laws. How about it?"

Her nostrils whitened with anger. "They have gall to show up here after—"

"What?" Greg cut in. His voice softened. "Maybe they can tell you. That's why I brought them. Like Hoskins said a few days ago, there's too much yelling and not enough listening."

"Get out!" Stern fairly yelled. He had changed to the repellant thing Greg had seen once before. He palmed his gun into his hand and lined it on Greg. "Turn around—all of you. Killers!"

Hoskins moved with a fat man's ponderousness between Amanda and Greg, wrapped his pudgy fingers around

117

Stern's gun muzzle and pushed it down. "It ain't your ranch or your say, Hal. Amanda?"

Greg's attention swung to her. She looked at Diana in the surrey. Diana sat with an unconcern and pride that even Greg could feel and he could also feel the powerful dislike playing back and forth between the two women. For them, all the others had vanished.

Greg spoke, instinctively breaking their illusion. "It's Vale Edwards you're all accusing. Can he have a say?"

His voice shook Amanda back to awareness of the rest of them. She looked blankly at Greg a moment and then nodded. Greg swung out of the saddle and walked to help Diana and her father to descend from the surrey. Diana sat unmoving.

"I'll stay here, Dad. I don't like to be where I'm not wanted."

Stern sneered, "Welcome you're not—and depend on it."

Greg swung around. "Is this your ranch, friend?"

Stern threw a look at Amanda, seeking support. Hoskins touched her shoulder. She bit at her lip and choked on the words. "Hal, they're invited to stay and talk."

She turned on her heel and strode back toward the shade trees. Greg helped Edwards out of the surrey. The old man threw off Greg's arm as quickly as he could, straightened and looked about at the men. Greg turned to Diana. She made a pout, then wrapped reins about the whipstock and accepted his hand to climb out.

She smoothed her skirt and touched her hair as Greg ground-tied the grays and then his own horse. Hoskins led the way to the shade of the trees. Edwards, accepting Diana's arm, slowly followed and Greg walked at their side. Behind them came Stern and the others.

Amanda waited for them. A circle of chairs had been drawn up for the conference. The man in the wheel chair

118

sat in rigid disdain and did not return Edwards', "Howdy, Wes. It's been a long time."

Edwards looked at Amanda. "I'm stove up and I ache at the joints. Believe me, that's the only reason I ask for a chair."

With a stabbing jerk of her arm, she indicated a chair. Edwards sank onto it and leaned back, checking an audible wince. Diana lifted her chin at Amanda's offer of a second chair and took a stand just behind him. The men slowly formed a big ring, unsure of themselves, eying Edwards as they would a cougar in their midst.

Greg felt the silent tension and spoke to Amanda with an ease he did not feel. "I don't know some of these gents, Miss Zane."

"No need to, Corwin. They're not friends."

He deliberately turned and slowly studied the men gathered around. There were perhaps a dozen of them, mostly ranchers but one or two obviously punchers doubling as foremen. They met his eyes with a quiet, hard challenge. Greg's gaze rested on Stern. "What did the sheriff say?"

"What do you figure Moyers'd say since he's Edwards' man?"

"That's not true," Edwards rumbled. "He was on my payroll but now he's a lawman and no more beholden to me than to anyone else. I'd like to get that straight right now."

The men shifted, throwing questioning glances at one another. Stern made a dry, sardonic sound. "That's hard to believe."

"It's true, but suit yourself."

Greg repeated. "What did the sheriff say?"

"That Sam Ralls was dead. He was shot in the back. Of course, we could see that for ourselves from the beginning, but we figured it was a good start for a greenhorn lawman."

Hoskins stepped up. "Hal, just tell it like it happened and

what Joe Moyers said. You ain't helping matters a bit the way you're talking."

The fat man had suddenly acquired a surprising firmness. Stern started to make a rejecting gesture, caught himself. "Will it do any good?"

"Try. Since Edwards is here, I don't think any of us want it said we didn't give him all the facts and a fair chance at his own say."

Stern shrugged. "All right. I'll start from the time I seen that Bar Y rider on Anchor range."

"Who was he?" Edwards demanded.

"I don't know his name. Seen him with your crew a couple of times. He was Bar Y, all right."

Stern told how he had found Ralls. He repeated the story of Ralls' dying statement. He told how he brought the body to the house and of Mary Ralls' collapse. The men stirred in angry discomfort and glared at Edwards, who sat unmoving and inscrutable. "Then I come here with the news," Stern finished.

Amanda smoothly took up the story. "Murder—backshooting is too much! I sent riders to the ranches. We decided to do something about it."

"You came to me," Greg cut in curtly, "wanting me to join your war."

She glared but, after a deep breath, said, "That's right. But we said we'd get the sheriff, stay within this bought-law in the Valley as long as we could. Well, we did."

"And Moyers said," Stern stepped forward, "he'd hunt down the killer, whoever he is. *Whoever*—get that? We know who it is by sight if not by name and we know who sent him to do the job. But Moyers, Bar Y's lawman, said there was no proof—nothing I saw was proof. Good God! what more do I need to see?"

"Anything else?" Edwards asked and they all swung in surprise to him. "Any other proof?"

120

Amanda whipped about. "Just what we know has been happening—burning, cattle rifled down, fences cut, people forced off their spreads or forced to sell out to you. Pressure on Ralls to sell and on Hobe Terrall. But now you don't have to buy Tumbling T, do you? It's on your side."

Edwards looked at her in admiration rather than anger. He slanted a look at the man in the wheel chair. "Your daughter has a lot of your fire and vinegar, Wes."

Wes Zane gripped the arms of the chair. "But not enough, Edwards, to say a Bar Y bullet crippled me—and you know it."

"No, Wes, I don't know it. And you know I never was a man to back-shoot or have another do a job for me."

He looked around the circle. "Before I was crippled and could ride, some of you called me friend. Now you call me devil. That's your right, I guess, but you could've come and asked me questions. Bar Y was—and is—open to you."

"With Bart Yates ramrodding a guncrew?" Stern demanded.

"Him—Bart Yates. He's the one you don't like," Edwards said. "Maybe I can understand. Bart's steel and push—and he's loyal. But that's not to the point now. Those burnings and such can come up later, too, except that I say now I had nothing to do with them—direct or through any orders I gave. Sam Ralls' killing—if a Bar Y man did it, I want him jailed and tried like anyone else. I'm telling Moyers that just in case you folks still have suspicions of him or me."

He looked slowly around the tight-faced group. "So if you decide to go to war against me, the weight's on you. I had nothing to do with any of these things. You have my word now and you needn't guess or suspicion. I reckon that's clear enough."

No one moved or spoke. Stern's eyes skittered from one face to another and Greg watched him, puzzled by the man's changing expressions. Edwards' knotted hands

121

gripped the edge of the straight chair in which he sat and he started to pull himself up.

"Big talk!" Stern scoffed. "Real big talk, but you haven't brought up a thing to prove what you're saying. You face Wes Zane and act sorry and holy. You say if a Bar Y man killed Sam, you'll see he pays for it. *If!* I say it was one of yours and I say you know about it. Or, maybe you figured from the start it was better not to know so you could stand up and give double talk like you just have."

Edwards froze, finger still gripping the seat. His mouth drew down as his eyes froze and Greg had a glimpse of the young fighting man who had long ago come into the Valley. Edwards slowly pulled himself up. He spoke evenly, softly. "Take what I said or leave it, Stern. As far as you're concerned, I don't give a damn one way or another. I never in my life bent to explain anything to your kind."

He started to turn but Stern took a lunging step and grabbed Edwards' open vest. Diana screamed. "No! Greg!"

Greg moved fast, hands descending on Stern's shoulders to whirl him about and away. Stern stumbled back, caught his balance and his hand snaked to his holster. He half drew the weapon but Amanda stepped between him and Greg as Hoskins, moving fast, grabbed Stern's wrist and forced the gun muzzle down into the holster.

Diana, at her father's side, appealed, "Greg, get us out of here. These awful people!"

Her blue eyes were deep pools of fright as she distractedly brushed a lock of red hair that had fallen over her forehead. She made an utterly feminine, helpless gesture toward Greg.

Amanda, watching first Diana and then Greg, flung her arm toward the gate and the surrey. "That's right, Corwin. Get your friend and your girl out of here. She is your girl, isn't she? Talk's had it that way since the fight in—"

Diana's angry screech drowned Amanda's words. Diana

sprang toward Amanda, a yellow-garbed fury with out-stretched, taloned hands. Before Amanda could turn, Diana's fingers were in her hair and she was jerked off balance. She blindly reached for Diana and fingers hooked into her dress. Cloth ripped along a shoulder and sleeve, ripped again.

Greg had a glimpse of white camisole and a pink ribbon worked through the neck. He glimpsed a shadow separating the rising curve of breasts and then everything blurred as the two women whirled about. Now Amanda clawed at Diana's face, caught a swirl of her hair above an ear. The bonnet jerked and dangled as hairpins flew and a bronze red cascade fell along Diana's cheek to her shoulder.

The fighting women fell and rolled in a flurry of dresses, petticoats and black-stockinged, kicking legs. One of them screamed in fury and the sound broke the paralysis that held the men. Greg, Hoskins and two others sprang forward. Greg grabbed a white shoulder half exposed through shreds of golden cloth. He pulled and tugged Diana half to her feet. But she reached for Amanda who, in turn, continued to battle. Hoskins and the second man pulled at her and Hoskins got a thick arm about her waist. Greg threw his arm about Diana and his muscles bunched as he pulled.

Suddenly the two women fell apart and the two groups stumbled back in opposite directions. The men caught their balance, still holding tightly to the straining women. Diana suddenly went limp in Greg's arms and she threw her hands over her face as she sobbed.

A few yards away, Amanda still struggled. "Let me go! She can't do this—!"

"Amanda!" Hoskins bellowed.

Diana whirled about, clinging to Greg and burying her face in his chest. Her bare shoulders shook and her whole body trembled. Amanda cried, "Get her out! This instant! I won't have her in my sight!"

Greg gently turned Diana away, looking over the tumble of red hair at Amanda. Her eyes met his in blazing anger. She had a long scratch down one cheek and her dress was ripped as badly as Diana's. Her lips moved spasmodically. "Get her out. Both of them. And take yourself with them!"

Greg moved Diana away with a curt bob of the head to Edwards. The march to the gate was silent except for Diana's jerking sobs. She walked, clinging to Greg and head down, for several yards. Then she became aware of her condition. She clutched at her falling hair, then realized the state of her clothing. She quickly crossed arms to cover her breasts, broke away from Greg and raced to the surrey.

She sat half crouched, vainly trying to pull shreds of dress back up to her shoulders as Greg came up with Edwards. She looked wildly at Greg, lips working but said nothing as he helped Edwards climb in. Greg turned to her, contrite. "Miss Diana, I didn't expect nothing like this. I'm sorry that—"

Her palm smacked across his face, flashing lights in his brain and bringing tears to his eyes. It passed in a second and her lovely, distracted face came back into focus.

"I hate you! I hate you!"

Greg involuntarily stepped back from the fury. Beyond her, Edwards painfully picked up the reins and said, "I'll drive a while. Best make yourself scarce in sight."

He made a head signal telling Greg to follow, wheeled the surrey around and rolled it out of the Rocking Chair yard toward the distant road.

124

XIV

When they reached the main road, Diana had managed to fix her hair in temporary order but there was very little she could do about the fight-ripped dress but hold it together at the shoulders. She acted as if Greg had completely disappeared. He looked back down the Rocking Chair road, empty of movement but for the ephemeral cloud of dust the surrey wheels had lifted. He followed after the vehicle, holding the bay down to the surrey's speed.

He wondered what surprise would develop in the next turn of events. Stern had called Edwards a liar to his face . . . Amanda and Diana were obviously irreconcilable enemies. How far could things fall apart or good intentions go wrong! Greg sighed, dismissing the problem with all its implications until he had more time to think it over.

He saw his own road far ahead and he spurred up to the surrey on Edwards' side. He bent down as the horses jogged along. "Maybe I'd best leave you here."

Diana spoke without turning her head. "That would be very nice."

Edwards said, "No, Corwin. I reckon you'd better listen to some questions and answers at Bar Y."

125

"Yates? You can do that without me. This is no time for him and me to be meeting."

"Nothing will happen on my ranch when you're there on my asking. I'll guarantee Bart for that. I'm beginning to see the value of a neutral man in this business. So you come along."

"Dad! Do you have to?"

"Yes, Missy, I do."

Greg looked hesitantly ahead to his nearing ranch road, dropped back to trail the surrey again. As he came to the road, he was of half a mind to wheel and ride out of this situation. But he couldn't. It had been his idea to get the Edwards and Zanes face to face. It had backfired and he was to blame, as he would have had credit had it worked. He continued after the surrey.

Not long after, they turned in the Bar Y road, threaded the hills and came out on the slope leading to the ranch itself. They were but a hundred or so yards clear of the hills when Greg saw a distant rider race toward them. The rider seemed hardly more than a moving, growing speck but Greg knew. He inwardly braced and warned himself to hold his temper in check.

Yates came speeding up, bent forward over the saddle. He straightened, hard eyes sweeping over the surrey, stabbing at Greg. Yates moved in to parallel the surrey. Greg deliberately dropped back to be out of range of voice.

Yates fired a series of questions and Greg saw him stare at Diana, who hunched her shoulders against it. He gestured back toward Greg, a violent fling of the arm. Edwards answered and Yates jerked erect as though struck. He started to argue but was silenced by a word and rode stiffly beside the vehicle as it moved down the slope and into the yard. Greg followed, slightly closing the distance.

Yates swung out of the saddle, darted around the surrey

to help Diana. But she shrank back. "No, Bart. Help Dad. I'm not—presentable."

His eyes lingered on her bare shoulders. She had again crossed her arms over herself and red crept into her cheeks. Yates' eyes skittered away as he wheeled about to reach Edwards just as the old man painfully touched one long leg to the ground. He grunted thanks for Yates' helping hand, turned as Greg dismounted. Diana jumped out of the surrey and raced toward the house in a flurry of ripped sunbright skirt.

Edwards said, "Bart, Corwin's here for a damn' good reason. There'll be no trouble between you."

"Vale, after what happened at Redman—"

"Bart! I mean it. If you can't speak civil to him, don't speak at all. And there'll be no fists or guns between you during the time he's here. Take that as an order, by God!"

Yates' face turned fury pale. He glared at Greg but answered, half choked, "All right, Vale. Just for now."

Vale clumped away, wincing with each step. Greg ground hitched the bay. Yates watched, expression baleful. Then he turned on his heel and caught up with Edwards and helped him across the porch.

Within the big room, Edwards glanced down a hallway then turned to the two men. He pointed to a cabinet. "Corwin, drinks over there. You need one . . . and pour one for me. You two stay right here. I'll be back after I see Diana."

He made a curt bob of the head and disappeared down the hall. Greg and Yates stood watching after him, avoiding one another. Then Greg tossed his hat on a nearby chair and walked to the cabinet, poured his drink. When he turned, he met Yates' black, hard eyes. The foreman said, "You keep piling up the tally against you. Now you've worked her into a fight."

"She got in her own. Edwards will tell you."

"Maybe. Main thing is I whipped you once before for

127

hanging around her. As soon as Vale cuts me loose, you're going to learn what a real beating is. Last time will be nothing."

Greg walked to a chair and sat down. He smiled tightly. "Just you and me for it? or will you need help again?"

Yates jerked toward him as his fists doubled, but he checked himself. "My boys forgot themselves. They won't again. Just you and me, Corwin."

"Name the time and place."

"That'll work out, friend. I'll see to it."

"So will I."

Yates moved to a window, looked out frowning and impatient. Greg finished his drink. The house grew silent. Edwards did not appear nor could Greg hear even the faintest sound of voices. Yates stirred, dropped into a chair. He glared at Greg but clasped powerful hands on his lap, saying nothing.

Edwards came slowly down the hallway, entered the room. He moved on to his own chair and torturously eased himself into it.

"Diana will be out in a few minutes. She's not full over her anger but at least she's thinking again. She's put the blame where it belongs."

Greg faintly smiled his relief. Yates asked, "What's this all about?"

"In a minute, Bart."

Silence stretched out through long minutes. Then Diana appeared. She had changed to the levis and blouse familiar to Greg and her hair was combed smoothly back, gathered by a narrow ribbon at the nape of her neck and allowed to cascade down her back.

She gave Greg an embarrassed look. "I'm sorry, Mr. Corwin. I was upset."

He came to his feet. "No need to be, ma'am. None of us figured on it."

Her vivid lips moved in a ghost of a smile and she sat down on a divan near her father. Yates' eyes followed her every move, cut venomously to Greg and then turned in question to Edwards. The old man shifted slightly and his knotted hands tightened with pain.

He told Yates why Greg had come and why he, Edwards, had agreed to go to Rocking Chair. He reviewed what had happened. Greg covertly watched Yates as the story unfolded. The man's face grew impassive after a first startled moment. Greg could tell nothing of what he thought.

Edwards gave an irritated sigh. "A lot of things were thrown at me, Bart, and I told 'em what I knew. Now I want to know what you know."

"No more'n you, Vale."

"Let's make sure. The next time I'm jumped, I want to be able to give dates and times and know where every Bar Y man was. So . . . Sam Ralls was back-shot. A Bar Y rider was seen near where he was killed and the man run off like he did it. Who was that man, Bart?"

"None of us," Yates instantly and flatly replied.

"It happened this morning sometime. Tell me where every manjack on Bar Y was."

Yates started ticking off on his fingers. "I rode out to north range with Tex, Joe and Dud. That's four. Bix and Curley . . ." He continued with the list of names. Greg listened but watched closely. Yates went through the list as though he unemotionally read a payroll. Locations, Greg noted, kept every man far from Anchor, ". . . Parker went after strays."

"Rocking Chair or Anchor way?"

"West only, Vale. No reason for him to be down that way."

Vale said after a moment, "Twenty head of beef were rifle-shot on Rocking Chair and the fence cut. I never heard about it but apparently you knew all the time. Why wasn't I told?"

Yates shrugged. "It didn't happen to us. Rocking Chair problem, so I figured, after our troubles, it was time someone else had 'em. Maybe I should'a told you."

"You should. Where was the crew?"

"Vale, you begin to sound like you suspicion me."

"I want facts, Bart. I had none to give when this was thrown in my face. I'm not going to be caught that way any more. So . . . ?"

Yates patiently went through the list of employees, locating them. This time most of the crew worked the draws to the east under Yates' personal supervision. He claimed the rest could be easily located here in the barns, corrals or in Redman.

Again, no one was near the scene of the slaughter. He spoke sincerely and convincingly and his expression did not belie his voice. Greg slanted a look at Diana, catching her eyes full on him. They swung away but not before he caught something speculative and—he hesitated but could not deny the thought—faintly admiring. It startled him and, for a time, he forgot Yates' continued listing.

Greg pulled his attention back to the man with an effort when Edwards asked about the burned line shacks. The answer was a repetition. Edwards then asked about the shooting to the south of the valley and Yates made the point that the ranch was close to broken country bounding the valley down that way. A wandering hardcase, a rustler—anything could have happened but nothing that could even remotely pin it on Bar Y.

"An accident worked for us," Yates finished. "It's part of our range now."

Greg covertly sought Diana. She sat demurely, eyes on her hands in her lap. But, as he watched, she lifted them, smiled faintly and looked away.

Edwards' voice brought Greg back to him. "All right, Bart. That's what I want to know. Sheriff Moyers will be around asking questions about Ralls' killing. Answer him straight and see to it everyone of our riders does the same thing. We're clean and we're going to stay that way."

Yates looked at Greg. "Only loose talk wandering over the Valley ever made it any other way, Vale. If it comes again, I'll know where it started."

Edwards frowned at the implication and, in answer, said to Greg, "You did us a favor . . . me, anyhow. I had no idea until today what was being said about Bar Y. I wanted you and Diana to hear what Bart had to say, since she's my daughter and you're caught up in the middle."

Greg stood up. "Too bad Stern or Hoskins—"

"Would they have come?" Edwards cut in.

"I guess not. But maybe I can spread the word somehow —Hoskins will at least listen. But right now the day's getting on and I'd best get back to—"

Diana interrupted. "No, Mr. Corwin. The least we can do is have you for supper. It will make up for . . ."

Her voice faded out but Greg understood. Yates made a low sound of anger. Greg shook his head but Diana said, "I insist, Mr. Corwin, and won't take no for an answer."

"That goes for me," Edwards assented. "Get things started in the kitchen, Missy, while we have a drink."

Diana smiled, turned its full power on Greg a second and then moved away across the room toward the kitchen. Edwards waved a hand toward the cabinet. "One of you pour a round, will you? I don't feel like moving."

Yates pulled himself out of his chair. "I pass this time, Vale. I reckon I should talk to the boys right away and best time would be at the cookshack when the whole crew's around." He glared at Greg. "Tell Diana to count me out."

Edwards shrewdly considered him. "You're right, Bart. But no drink? Sure?"

"Not now, anyhow."

Yates swung around Greg and strode from the room. The

131

heavy door slammed and Edwards, shifting painfully, said, "You two will lock horns for sure. Wish it could be another way."

Greg walked to the cabinet, picked up a bottle. "Things work out funny sometimes."

"Diana—ain't it?"

Greg filled the shot glasses and carried them back to Edwards. "Yates figures it that way."

"But you've not even looked at her?"

"No man could help looking. But I've got no business doing any more than that and I know it. Here's to your health, sir."

"I need it." Edwards lowered the half-filled shot glass. "Like her mother, Diana deserves the best but who in hell am I to know what *she* considers best? She makes her own choice when the time comes."

"Someone will be lucky."

"I figure that way but, then, she's my daughter." He abruptly asked, "How does Tumbling T shape up now that you've had a chance to dig your spurs into it?"

They talked range and ranch problems and the old man gave Greg pointers out of his long experience. Now and then they heard muted noises from behind the closed door leading to the dining room and kitchen beyond. Diana finally appeared to cut across the room to the hallway.

"Supper soon?" Edwards asked.

"Soon. I have to change. This is no proper dress for a lady with a guest."

She disappeared into a bedroom. Edwards lifted his empty glass and Greg refilled it as well as his own. Edwards accepted his drink and nodded a leonine head toward the lamps. "Mind lighting 'em? Getting toward dusk. Diana's primping and Ah Fong's jumping to her orders back in the kitchen."

Greg lit the big lamps, whose cheerful glow dimmed the

final shreds of day outside the windows. He turned from the lamps in time to see Diana disappear into the dining room. He had a glimpse of gray silk and a red curl hanging down behind a small ear.

She reappeared after another long wait, throwing the door wide. "It's ready and I'm starved!"

She stood framed with lamplight behind her, accenting her figure. She had a glow that Greg had not noticed before, and it seemed her lips were a richer color, her skin softer. Faint shadows cast by the lamps heightened the delicate shape of cheekbones and deepened the eyes beneath the brows. She wore the gray gown Greg had glimpsed, the V-neck low, framing a golden chain and locket.

He became aware Edwards watched him with an ill suppressed smile. Diana helped her father as the three of them went into the dining room where a Chinaman in black jacket placed a final dish, made a jerking bow and hurried into the kitchen.

Greg had a confusing meal in that sensations followed and flowed into one another. Above all, was the beautiful woman who sat across the table. There was the food, excellent and much of it. There was the easy talk. There was the satisfying bite of hot, strong coffee and apple pie afterward.

Then they returned to the main room and Edwards dropped into his chair. Diana stood hesitant before him. "Why can't we sit out on the porch? It's a lovely night."

"Not for me, now that I'm anchored," Edwards remonstrated. "Too much trouble working myself up again."

She turned to Greg. "You, Mr. Corwin?"

"Go ahead," Edwards grunted to them. "Me, I'm happy right here."

Greg followed Diana as she walked out onto the dark porch. She crossed it to stand at the top of the steps, looking out into the night. Greg stood uncertainly just behind her.

She looked up over her shoulder. The light from the window revealed her smile.

"Mind a stroll, Mr. Corwin?"

She moved down the steps without waiting for a reply. He walked beside her out into the yard and along a faintly discernible path to the fence and drive gate. The night was moonless but the stars were many and brilliant. A faint breeze stirred leaves high above in the dark silhouettes of trees.

They came to the fence and Diana turned along it in a direction that wheeled the house between them and the other buildings. She broke the silence. "I treated you badly on the way home today."

"I figure you had a right to after what happened."

"But you couldn't have known it would."

He chuckled. "That's certain. I begin to believe what they tell me about Amanda Zane. Spitfire, that one!"

They now strolled some distance from the house. Diana asked, "Do you see her often?"

"Amanda? No."

Diana's pace slowed. "You like her?"

"I guess so, though everytime I meet her there's trouble."

Diana moved into the shadow of a tree and leaned against it. Her face appeared to Greg as a soft white blur, her body a lighter, curvesome shadow against the darker, solid shape of the tree. She looked toward the distant hills and Greg waited, aware of her but uncertain what to do.

"And what do you think of me? Or is that too bold a question?"

Greg peered through the half light but could not read her face. "I like you."

"And everytime *we've* met you've had trouble?"

"Well . . . not like Amanda Zane, I'll say that."

"I'm glad."

She had subtly eased away from the tree and stood within

134

arm's reach, her face, framed by the dark aura of her hair, lifted to his. Greg felt his throat constrict but he tightly held himself in check.

He sensed a pout in her voice. "You like her better."

"I didn't say that."

Now he could almost feel her soft breath on his cheek. He choked down a hunger born of long-time loneliness and sharpened by immediate desire. Her voice dropped almost to a whisper.

"I've wondered. You never look at me, really."

"I—"

He swept her into his arms and she came willingly. She pressed close, her lips clinging for a long, long moment. He had the scent of her hair and a faint perfume in his nostrils and the feel of a soft, mobile mouth against his. His arms tightened.

But her elbows levered against him and she stepped away, breathing deeply. She touched her hair, threw a look at the house. He tentatively reached for her but she smoothly avoided his arm. She said in a gusty whisper, "We'd best get back to the house. Dad—or Bart . . ."

The name shocked him into alarmed clarity. If just talking to this girl on the street of Redman had caused a mauling fight, what would these last few moments set in motion? He peered at her as he turned beside her and started back along the fence toward the house. Had that embrace and kiss been really for him? Or was she playing with Yates' jealous love?

Feeling his intent gaze, she turned her head and smiled as her fingers lightly touched his cheek. "That was sweet, Greg. But very bold, wasn't it? and dangerous? We really must watch ourselves."

He merely nodded. Now they could see the corner of the distant bunkhouse and cookshack, the windows aglow with lamplight. He could not be sure at the distance, but thought that darker shadows of loafing, watching men broke the smooth plane of dark buildings. Yates among them? He looked again at Diana.

Now light from the house close by fell fully on her. She showed no sign of inner disturbance. Her smooth face hid what emotions might have ruled her a few moments ago. Perhaps that was so. She kissed as the fancy struck her. Flirt?

When Greg rode out of the dark yard less than an hour later, he still did not know. He rode out with senses alert and tense. But Bart Yates did not appear out of the night shadows.

Still, Greg did not ride easily until he was through the hills and knew the main valley road was not far ahead.

XV

A single light glowed from the bunkhouse when Greg approached his own home and he had no more than trotted up to the corral than Cal Weber appeared. "You been gone a long time. Need supper?"

"Had it, but a drink will sit fine. And I want to talk to you. Come in the house."

Seated in the small office, Greg told what he had done, Cal listening round-eyed. When he finished, the old man shook his head. "You do the damnedest things! No one else'd have the guts."

"Not guts—just a sensible way to get at the truth. It didn't work. Stern called Edwards a liar to his face."

"And that made Edwards madder'n ever?"

"Edwards didn't know what was going on—or maybe I should say not all of what was going on. I believe him. Oh, he went away from Rocking Chair mad enough, but remember he called in Yates and grilled him."

"And Yates cleared himself."

"Sounds that way, but I noticed every time something happened, Yates and some of the crew were working out on the range. Not in sight, so far as I can tell."

137

"He lied then?"

"I don't know. But no one can vouch for him but his own crew."

"And *he* hired every manjack of 'em."

"Even if it's so, where does it leave us? And why should Yates start a range war when there's nothing coming to him but Bar Y pay?"

Cal shrugged. "I give up. But main thing is, what do we do now?"

"Stand hitched and watching." Greg stood up, started to leave the room with Cal but stopped suddenly at the door. "Sam Ralls is dead. Who gets Anchor?"

"His wife, Mary, I'd guess. But I doubt if she can run it."

"No one saw him shot, either."

"Meaning?"

"I don't know. Leastways not tonight. It's been a long day and I'd rather hit a bunk than figure that one out."

The next morning, Greg and Cal started the daily routine of breakfast and laying out work for themselves. But when they had saddled their horses, mounted and turned toward the north range, Greg reined in. Cal looked about, surprised. "What now?"

"How do I get to Anchor?"

"Hey now, what—?"

"Keeps nagging and bothering and, besides, I should pay neighborly respects."

"If they'll let you," Cal grumbled but he gave the directions. "Clean down to the south end of the valley. By the time you ride, visit and come back, it'll be day-end sure."

"Then you're in charge of Tumbling T. See you come night."

Greg reined about and rode off, leaving Cal to stare after him then shake his head and ride slowly toward his work.

Greg had come into the Valley from the south but by a different route, so he saw this part of the range for the first

138

time after he passed the Rocking Chair turn-off. He gave that road a regretful look and rode on. The country beyond was of a piece with the rest of the valley except that the high mountains bounding it loomed ever more grim.

The miles passed. The mountains literally towered over the trees and Greg, their illusory distant smoothness giving way to broken slopes, crags and dark canyons. Then Greg saw the Anchor sign. The main road ended here almost at the foot of the peaks. That meant there was no pass suitable for a road through them.

The ranch road now paralleled the peaks at least a mile out from their base. It plunged into a small forest, made a sharp turn toward the mountains and burst free of trees into a grassland that continued on to the broken country. He saw the Anchor buildings.

A small spread and not a wealthy one, Greg judged, yet corrals, barns and outbuildings looked sturdy and well kept. The main house was a squat, long structure with high field-stone chimneys at either low-gabled end. The yard looked trim and he saw the bright color of flowers in beds about the house.

He had almost reached the house when its door opened and a woman stepped out. She shaded her eyes as she peered toward Greg. At a distance, he noted the black dress broken by a big white apron.

As he drew closer, the indistinct figure resolved into that of a woman of medium height, a bit plump. When he hitched the bay to the fence post and walked to her, he saw that her raven hair had streaks of gray over the ears. She was pretty in the way women are whom age has just started to touch. But he also noted the strain about the mouth, a puffiness below the eyes that spoke of weeping.

He took off his hat. "Mrs. Ralls, ma'am?"

"Yes."

"I'm Greg Corwin. I bought Tumbling T a spell back.

139

Word came about—what happened here and I'd like to give my respect and condolences."

Her chin trembled then firmed. "I've heard of you. It surprises me you've come."

"You heard wrong then, ma'am. I never met your husband, of course, but . . ."

They stood in awkward silence as she studied him with soft brown eyes. Then she sighed. "I think you come on a kindly act, Mr. Corwin. I'll take it so."

"Thank you. I'd hoped you would."

"He's inside. Funeral's not 'till tomorrow. Do you want to see him?"

Greg hesitated a second but realized the offer meant at least a temporary acceptance. He nodded and she smiled wanly. "Come in, then."

She preceded him to the door. He stepped into a narrow hallway running the length of the house, doors opening off it to either side. She made a gesture. "In the parlor. This way."

A few moments later he stood before a plain coffin supported by sawhorses, ill hidden by black muslin. The small room looked crowded, furniture pushed back to the walls and dim because of a pulled shade at the single window. The coffin loomed gigantic in so small a space. Greg noted the little bouquets of flowers, obviously garnered from the beds outside by the woman standing just beside and behind him.

He looked down on Sam Ralls, a waxen figure in a stiff white shirt and black suit. There was no sign on the lifeless, smooth face of the agony of smashing slugs. He had been a short, box of a man with powerful shoulders and thick arms.

Greg stood for the time he felt needful to pay the usual range country respects to the dead. Then he said in a whisper, "I figure he was a good man."

140

Mary Ralls caught a sob in her throat and her eyes misted. "He was, Mr. Corwin. Hard working, fair and honest. Had no time to enjoy himself and that's the shame of it. He might've if he hadn't been—"

She openly cried. Greg gently touched her arm, turned her toward the door and they walked out into the hall and on to the porch. She had recovered somewhat by the time they stood looking out over the valley, Greg, judging her first, asked, "How did it happen?"

"Why, I figure everyone knowed. Hal spread the word."

"A word gets changed, ma'am, as it's passed from one person to another."

"Yes, that's true. Poor Sam got up that morning as usual . . ." She entered into a long, detailed description of everything her husband had done. Greg listened patiently, understanding. "Him and Hal were together when it happened. Hal told me first thing he heard was the shots and then Sam was dead."

"Hal was with him? not nearby?"

"Rode out with him. Stayed with him." She indicated a low hill, far out. "See that kinda notch off-side that hummock 'way over there? Right beyond it. Sam had spotted a wandering, wobbly calf and he worried about its mommy. So him and Hal rode out to find the cow."

She rambled on, telling how she had worked here at the house the whole time her husband was being killed, how Hal Stern came in with the body. Greg listened just as patiently as she told of the gathering of the little ranchers, the coming of the sheriff. She finished with a snort, "Sheriff Moyers looked around but he ain't about to find anything against Bar Y!"

Greg assured her, "One way or another, we'll find the killer, Mrs. Ralls. I have to be getting back home now. Funeral's tomorrow, you say? In Redman?"

"Yes. Sam never wanted no burying here on Anchor. Said

141

there was always a chance it'd fall into strange hands and they'd not care about the dead, if there was any. Tomorrow, right after noon."

"Thank you. I aim to be there."

"For a stranger, you're kind to my Sam. You ain't at all what I'd come to think, hearing the others talk about you."

"I hope not." He indicated the distant hill. "Mind if I ride over that way?"

"Sure not! I made Hal take me to the very spot. Head straight north about half a mile out from the off-spur of the hummock. You'll see a lone tree. Just beyond and to the left."

He mounted the bay and swung around, cantered out of the yard with a touch of fingers to hat brim to the woman on the porch. He headed toward the distant hillock, the one with the notch.

Beyond the hill, he headed due north as Mary Ralls had told him. The ground sloped gently down into a great, wide shallow swale. He saw the lone tree far ahead. He pulled up into its shade a moment, then cast out, bearing to the left. He watched the ground for sign.

He came on single tracks and then a whole area where horses had stood, moved about, cut out and in. In the center of the rough circle of smashed grass and tracks, he saw black, dried blood caked on ground and grass. Sam Ralls had fallen here and died.

Greg reined in, eased to a slouch as his eyes slowly made a circuit of the surrounding area. Except for the tree behind him, bushes and more trees at least a mile northward, there was nothing to break the sweep of grass.

Shot twice in the back, Greg remembered Hal Stern's statement, but no suspicious rider could have possibly slipped up on Ralls unseen. Man and horse would stand out like the distant mountains. The far bushes? No—a Colt

142

could not be accurate at that distance. Yet the slugs were placed in the middle of Ralls' back.

Greg twisted about to look back toward the house, invisible now, and he recalled what Mrs. Ralls had said. He thought about it, working his lips, then straightened and reined the horse about.

As he approached the hummock, Hal Stern appeared riding toward him. Greg reined in but Stern came on at an even pace. As he drew up, his expression was withdrawn, neither suspicious nor friendly. He thumbed his hat back from his forehead.

"Mary said you'd come to pay respects and rode up this way. Find anything?"

"Nothing."

"Figures—none of us did. Just Sam laying there, dead."

"Dead? I thought he spoke to you—"

"He did. Last breath. Didn't mean laying dead that way."

"Where'd you run onto the Bar Y rider before you found Sam?"

Stern pointed. "Maybe half a mile beyond those bushes and trees over there. Sam and me hunted for a stray calf and its mommy we saw up this way. He covered this swale and I took a look-see over there."

"Too bad you didn't stay with him."

"Ain't that so! He might be alive."

"Colt slugs, I think you said."

"That's right. Close up, too."

"Sam didn't know what or who hit him, I reckon," Greg suggested.

"Figures that way."

Greg said, "How'd the meeting end the other day?"

"That was a damn' fool thing for you to do, bringing the Edwards!"

"They had their side. I figured you should hear it."

"We did—and we don't believe it."

143

"Is that what you decided after—I left?"

"Well . . . mostly. We're going to fight. But we figured to wait for two things. First, see if Sheriff Moyers will cover up Bar Y, despite what Edwards said. Second, we figure Bar Y will make a move. Edwards tried to soft-talk us so we'd shut our eyes and be all set up when he hits."

"Suppose Edwards was speaking truth—on both counts?"

"Well, Corwin, we leave you to swallow his bait. By the way, Mary says you'll be at the funeral."

"That's right. But right now I'd better be getting back to Tumbling T."

Stern fell in beside Greg as he started back toward the house. Some distance out, Greg veered off toward the ranch road, spoke a farewell word that Stern answered with a nod and grunt. Aware of the man behind him, Greg touched the bay into a trot and started the journey home.

The next day, Cal and Greg rode into Redman. It may have been imagination, but Greg felt a subdued air to the town and that business traffic around the square was light. As Cal and Greg passed a saloon hitchrack, the old man pointed to the brands on several of the horses.

"Bar Y. What brought them to town? Reckon they plan some trouble at the funeral?"

"I doubt it."

"Wouldn't put it past 'em. In there likkering up and then later . . . You can figure Bart Yates for anything."

They stopped at one of the town's cafes for the noon meal. Afterwards, they strolled about the square and neared the bank, the one imposing brick structure in the town. Greg remembered Unger and his offer, and he looked closely at the windows but did not see the banker. They strolled on but Greg looked back at the bank, trying to catch a nebulous idea lurking at the edge of his mind.

Cal looked up at the courthouse clock. "About time we

144

went out to the cemetery. Everyone should be there by now."

"Didn't see them come through town."

"No one does, going to the cemetery. Direct road along the east edge of town."

They returned to the hitchrack before the cafe and then rode slowly eastward, away from the square. They turned north at the last road and, far ahead, on a small knoll, Greg saw the lonely high gates of the cemetery breaking a low stone wall.

They rode up the slope and entered the gates. Then Greg saw the gathering of buckboards, buggies and saddled horses over to the right, a group of people, backs to him. Greg and Cal moved slowly down the road. As they approached, a few turned to see who came up. Above the heads of the others, Greg saw the preacher and Mrs. Ralls' bowed, veiled head, Hal Stern standing bareheaded beside her. The preacher spoke the burial ceremony in sonorous tones.

Greg started to dismount, froze in surprise when he saw a familiar surrey. Vale and Diana Edwards sat in it, the old man's head bared. Greg caught Diana's glance and smile, then she sobered and looked away.

Greg slowly dismounted. Cal had seen them, too. He started to ask a question but Greg quickly shook his head. He moved to the rear of the group about the grave and listened for some moments as he cast around the faces he could see. Most were strangers. Some he had seen at the disastrous meeting at Rocking Chair, Hoskins among them. If any of them were aware of the Edwardses, they did not reveal it.

Greg slanted a look toward the surrey. It was as near the grave as the road would permit, but obviously apart and not accepted by the people about the grave. Greg's roving eyes held on a face, puzzled a moment, until he recognized

Tex of Bar Y. The man stood apart and some distance from the surrey. He wore belt and gun and stood at such an angle that he could counter any attack against Vale Edwards.

Greg bared his bowed head with the rest when the sonorous voice called for prayer. It lasted for some time and then the "Amen" rolled over the group. The final lines of the ceremony followed and even Greg heard the dull hollow sound of clods striking the coffin in the grave.

The group broke up and Mrs. Ralls came sobbing and leaning on Stern's arm. Also supporting her, walked Amanda Zane, subdued, sorrowful, but with a set of delicate jaw that bespoke anger. She saw Greg. Her eyes rounded then she moved on without a word.

Hoskins came then, saw Greg and swung around to stand beside him. He said in a low voice, "Glad you came."

"Thanks. Can you say the same for Edwards over there?"

"In a way. Don't know about the rest."

They fell silent as passing men and their wives eyed Greg, some with curiosity, some with a flat, silent rejection. Buggies wheeled about on the road. Horses tossed heads as men caught up the reins and mounted. Within five minutes no one remained but Hoskins, Greg, Cal, the Edwards and Tex and a cemetery worker who stood waiting with a spade beside the mound of brown earth.

Greg turned to the surrey as Edwards lifted the reins. Tex, over to the side, wheeled about and Greg sensed the man's tension. Edwards waited, saying, "Howdy, Corwin."

"Glad you came, sir."

"You're the only one."

"How do you do, Mr. Corwin?" Diana leaned beyond her father and smiled. It was friendly but impersonal, giving no hint of the kiss by the tree or the supple body close against him.

Hoskins said, "Beg pardon, Vale. I'm glad, too."

"Well, that's something." Edwards indicated the grave with a dip of the whip. "I liked Sam Ralls. I could've said

146

that to the rest until I choked and they still wouldn't believe me. But coming like this . . ."

"Makes the point," Greg finished as the old man's voice faded off.

Edwards turned to Hoskins. "Tell your friends I'm seeing Moyers. He'll be sheriff in this business and nothing else."

"I'll tell 'em."

Edwards touched the team with the tip of the whip. Greg and Hoskins stepped back as the surrey rolled by, made a sharp turn and moved off through the cemetery gates. Tex rode after the surrey.

Hoskins, watching the surrey until it disappeared down the slope, finally sighed. "Corwin, you know what's wrong here? There ain't nobody anyone else can trust—no go-between that Edwards or my bunch wouldn't figure has something to gain. Not even you."

"I've tried, God knows!"

"Sure. But . . . when you bought Tumbling T, you lined up with us like any small rancher. Now we figure you got something to gain from Bar Y. Not that it's so. It's just everything's all black and white and nothing in between. I swear, both Bar Y and us would trust a Redman bartender before we would each other."

The idea that lurked at the rim of consciousness suddenly clicked. Greg's face lighted and he dropped his hand on Hoskins' beefy shoulder. "Thanks! Cal, let's get back to town."

He turned on his heel, leaving the two men with open mouths. Cal recovered and hurried after Greg who jumped into the saddle and impatiently waited for the old puncher. The moment Cal's rump hit leather, Greg spurred out along the cemetery road.

Cal caught up with him as they neared the first houses of the town. "What bit you?"

Greg shouted over the roll of hoofs. "Something like peace in Sioux Valley. At least a chance!"

147

XVI

＊＊＊＊

Despite the ready smile, Greg sensed reserve in Fred Unger as the banker waved him to a chair beside the desk.

"Good to see you again, Corwin. I hope this means business for my bank. But—if this is about the offer I made—the situation has changed. Things are coming to a head."

Unger's smile remained warm and open, suggesting honest regret that he must now act as banker rather than drinking companion. Greg had shaped the words of his appeal but caution warned that, first, there was something here he needed to know.

So he assumed a frown. "What would interest you?"

"Well, hard to say. I'd like to do business with you. Still—this is a bank and . . . I can't top Bar Y's offer by very much, if at all. I warned you not to let time go by."

"But what's the difference? No war yet."

"With Sam Ralls murdered, the war's on! It's just that the guns haven't yet started popping. I hear things from both sides. So, say two thousand over Bar Y's offer to Hobe Terrall? And that's generous, believe me."

"You hear from both sides?"

148

"Of course, both sides talk to me. I'm their banker."

"Fine!" Greg hitched forward and Unger's brows drew down in a disconcerted frown. "You're just the man I'm looking for. Up at the cemetery, Hoskins said his friends and Bar Y would trust a Redman saloonkeeper quicker'n they would one another. Suspicion between 'em, so neither side can talk honest. But you—"

"Now, wait—"

Greg brushed aside the interruption. "Both sides do business with you and they both talk to you. So you could act as peacemaker."

"Not a chance in the world!"

"Every chance! Edwards is in town right now, I think. So's Hoskins and Amanda Zane and maybe Mrs. Ralls and Hal Stern, unless they went directly back to Anchor. We could get them all together. They might suspicion one another but they won't suspicion you."

"Now what could I do?"

"You know the story—the way both sides tell it. You know most of it's misunderstanding. You could clear that up. In a week Sioux Valley could be peaceful again."

"I'm not so sure, Corwin."

"You won't even try?"

Unger steepled his hands and pursed his lips. "I didn't say that. Depends. Let me think it over."

"Everyone's in town. *Now* is the time."

Unger smiled with sardonic wisdom. "Is it? Sam Ralls just laid to rest and you want the Ralls and Zanes to shake hands with Edwards when they think he's back of the murder? It's not time."

Greg reluctantly conceded. "Say you're right. Then, when?"

"I don't know. Maybe never, the way things go now. Don't get the idea I'm trying to slide out of something if it's worth

149

the time and effort. That's the point. Let me decide. Now
. . . about Tumbling T—"

"Still not for sale."

"But I thought—"

"Sorry. I didn't have that on my mind at all—just this other
thing."

"Well, in that case—" Unger stood up and extended his
hand. "We can't do business, can we? As to being a peacemaker—let me decide."

"Time's running out—like you warned me about Tumbling T."

Greg walked into the main room and Cal joined him as he
strode out through the door to the street. Turning sharply,
Greg glanced in the bank window as he passed to see Unger
at the near end of the line of cages. As he caught Greg's look
he sharply turned away.

"Now what'd you do?" Cal asked as they walked on along
the square.

"Nothing, damn it!" He told Cal of his idea and of Unger's
hesitation. "He's the right man to do it and that leaves me
wondering why he waits."

"You tried to brand him too fast. Now, me, was I in his
shoes, I don't know as I'd want to jump heels first into
trouble."

"What trouble for him? They'd at least listen to a man
who holds their mortgages or loans them money. Vale Edwards does business with Unger, so he must respect him."

Cal thumbed his hat back from his high, sunburned forehead. "Don't keep asking me. How would I know how a
banker thinks?"

They came to the saloon where the Bar Y horses had
been hitched but now the rack was empty. Further on Greg
turned in the General Store. Without thought or glance to
who might be in the store, he went to a counter and asked
for both Colt and rifle cartridges. The clerk stacked the

150

boxes on the counter and Greg pulled out his leather poke to pay.

Cal made a strange sound behind him and Greg wheeled to face Amanda Zane. Her dark eyes silently lashed him, swung to the cartridge boxes, back to him.

"Preparing for war, Mr. Corwin?"

"Supply's low, that's all."

She made a mock study of the purchase. "Better buy more, Mr. Corwin. You'll need 'em, since you're siding with Bar Y."

Greg slapped coins on the counter, said to Cal, "Have them tied up and put 'em in the saddlebags."

Cal saw the pinched, white color about Greg's nostrils and hastily moved away with the clerk. Amanda started to turn. "You're a fool, Amanda Zane."

She whipped around. "Fool! Me?"

"You—and everyone else in the valley."

"Except you, of course."

"I'm beginning to think so. Everyone is so busy hating and suspicioning everyone else, there's no time to think."

"Indeed!" Greg became aware that the store had become completely silent and that customers and clerks listened, frozen where they stood. Amanda's scorching voice licked at him. "I can think of Sam Ralls murdered by a Bar Y bullet."

"That's just a fool wanting things to be his way."

Her arm swung up, palm open for a ringing slap. He caught her wrist and they stood, eye to eye, both anger shaken. He demanded, "How do you *know!* Hal Stern's word? A cold trail out in that swale? Did you look around? Were you even there?"

"I was there!"

"Did you use your eyes? Have you talked to the sheriff?"

She wrenched her hand free, angrily rubbing her wrist. "Moyers! You know who he works for."

"I asked if you'd talked to him—you or any of your hell-bent-for-war friends."

"No!"

"Afraid to? He's just across the street in the courthouse."

"He could be right beside me and—"

"You'd be afraid to ask. It might stampede to nothing all those hates you've stored up." He towered over her. "Damned big of all of you to give the sheriff a chance—on your terms, and provided you don't find out what he's done or even believe him. Think? Is that what you call it?"

They stood immobile, their eyes locked. She became aware of the rest of the store and her glance flicked to either side. Greg smiled thinly. "Yes, they're hearing everything. Still won't go with me to the sheriff?"

"Damn you!" she breathed under her breath. Her head and chin lifted and her voice reached to the rear of the big room. "Of course I will, even if it's a waste of time."

He stepped aside, giving her an unobstructed path to the door. She swept by him, skirt swinging and straight, slender back speaking her dudgeon. Greg walked just behind her until they came out on the walk, then he moved up beside her.

She shrunk away from his hand to assist her off the wooden sidewalk into the dirt street. They moved toward the courthouse. Beyond the reach of the ears of the curious who had followed as far as the door and the walk behind them, she said in a low, tight voice, "I don't appreciate this, Mr. Corwin."

"I don't appreciate murder and bullets so I'll do anything to end 'em."

"You're just breeding more, throwing in with Bar Y."

Abrupt set of jaw and pull of mouth showed his impatience and disgust. They crossed the street and moved to the courthouse. Amanda turned sharply away from the main entrance, along a walk that led to a side door. Greg saw the

152

sheriff's sign. He opened the door for her and she swept in ahead of him.

Except that it was in the courthouse itself, the office was like many Greg had glimpsed down in Colorado and in a dozen cowtowns. Big room with bare scuffed floor, a rack in which rifles were stacked and locked, a wall filled with reward and wanted dodgers, a few heavy and uncomfortable wooden chairs. A desk, massive and scuffed almost as badly as the floor.

A man behind it scrambled to his feet in surprise as he recognized Amanda. Shrewd, clear gray eyes threw a searching look at Greg. The man said in a pleasant, deep voice, "Miss Zane, I'm surely surprised."

Her eyes flashed about the room, taking in the barred door behind the desk leading to a small cell block, touched on the bars across the outer office windows and then the empty chairs as though she expected to find Bar Y riders occupying them.

Greg said, "We want to know if anything's turned up on the Ralls business, and all the other things that've been happening."

Moyers asked, "And you're—?"

"Corwin, new owner of Tumbling T."

"Pleased to meet you. I've had word of you."

He extended his hand, leaning big and powerful body over the desk. Greg judged jaw, chin, face and head that gave the impression of granite, the broken nose slightly out of line along the high bridge. Face and body and strong grip of fingers marked rugged strength and toughness that the crooked mouth's surprisingly soft smile belied. The star on his open black vest glittered as he dropped Greg's hand and hastily circled the desk to pull up a chair for Amanda.

"Thank you," she said with an edge of ice, "though I doubt if you're very long telling us what you've found."

Moyers let a flick of anger touch mouth and jaw. Greg

pulled up a second chair with deliberate noise and dropped into it. Moyers waited, silent. Amanda stood a long moment and then, with a flounce, dropped into the seat. Moyers returned to this desk and slowly sat down.

Amanda attacked. "I suppose Bar Y has told you what to look for?"

"Why, yes, for that matter. You just missed Vale Edwards. He told me to look for every sign, question everyone, and that means Bart Yates and Vale's crew. It means Hal Stern and you and your father. Maybe you, Corwin."

"What little I know you're welcome to."

Amanda said, "Bar Y last, of course, Moyers, so the killer can have time to get out of the country."

Moyers folded powerful hands on the desk. He spoke as evenly as before. "Get this straight, Miss Zane. I once worked for Vale but now I work for the badge. I owe nobody anything. As a matter of fact, I've already been to Bar Y and checked every puncher and person. They told me where they were and what they were doing about the time Ralls was killed."

Amanda recovered from her fluster and commented scornfully, "All far away from Anchor, I'd bet."

"So they say."

"So, that's that." She started to rise. "Case closed."

"Sit down, Miss Zane." He gave the command softly but she slowly sank back. Then her black eyes flamed at the thought of her surrender. Before she could protest, Moyers said, "I listened and tallied. I don't believe or disbelieve. I'm checking. I'll be checking Hal Stern—and your crew—and your Cal Weber and you, Corwin. I'll question Mary Ralls when it's decent time to do it. I'll question Hoskins, everyone. And then I'll check and check again. I liked Sam Ralls, everyone did—except one. I want that one back in there waiting for trial."

He nodded toward the cell block. "As for the other things—

your father's shooting. I want to talk to him again about it. He saw someone ride off on what he believes to be a Bar Y horse."

"He didn't lie!"

"That he didn't. But he branded Bart Yates. Maybe Bart did it, hard as that is to believe. But maybe he did. Still, Wes Zane can't take oath that he saw Bart's face, can be?"

Amanda moved uncomfortably and grudgingly answered, "No, but his back and—"

"Ma'am, how many Sioux Valley men would look like Bart Yates, same build and all—from the back? Suppose Hoskins was shot the same way and he glimpsed a back like —well, Corwin's or your father's. Should I arrest them, charge them with murder just on that?"

He waited and, as her silence continued, he asked softly, "Should I?"

She forced out, "I—guess not."

"Now—Sam Ralls. No one saw the shooting. Hal saw a man before it happened. I'm riding to Anchor and I want Stern to go with me to Bar Y and pick that man out. Fair enough?"

"Why didn't you do that before?"

"Sam dead and Mary broke up? No one but Hal to handle things—the funeral and all? You and your friends were with me when I rode out to Anchor right after the killing, Miss Zane. You and your friends were with me when I looked over the swale where Sam was shot. You were with Mary that day. There's just Hal to run things. Was that the time to drag him off?"

She shook her head and found that her twisting fingers needed close study. Greg said, "I went to Anchor myself and looked things over."

Moyers swung his big head in a silent question that Greg answered. "You looked at Ralls? . . . Did he have powder burns?"

"Yes."

"Long shooting for powder burns."

Moyers' mouth flicked and tightened in silent words of caution. He turned to Amanda. "I'm trying to catch a killer and do a job of lawing. Give me a chance."

She started at his sudden, quiet appeal. "We decided to do that, within reason."

"Time you mean. Who sets the limit—you people? Me? Or the killer trying to keep out of sight?"

"I don't know. I never thought of it that way."

Moyers stood up, smiled. "I'm glad you came, Miss Zane. Maybe we're a little closer on understanding—at least about my job. Come in any time you want to ask questions and tell your friends to do the same." He looked at a yellow-faced clock on the wall. "I just got time to ride to Anchor."

Amanda and Greg also stood up. Moyers held out his hand and Amanda, with a faint hesitation, accepted it. Greg followed her out of the building and they stopped in common accord to look across the busy square. Greg noted her frown, the underlip held lightly between her teeth.

"Could we have made a mistake—I mean about Bar Y?"

"Might have. Again you could be right. Who knows?"

"I think we *thought* we knew." She looked back toward the sheriff's office. "He's thorough—if he's telling the truth."

"Any reason why he shouldn't?"

"Well . . . once worked for Bar Y."

"That sticks in all your craws, like you figure I can't mind my own business and want peace with all my neighbors."

Color swept her face and she studied him, dark eyes searching deep. "How can we know?"

"No way I can tell you how, except maybe to say suspicion and fact don't always go together. But I can't ride herd on suspicions running wild."

She studied him a moment more. "I'm going home and your spread's on the way. I'd not mind company as far as

156

Tumbling T road. That is, could you wait until I get the buggy loaded at the store?"

"I can wait. Meet you—?"

"Half an hour. There's the buggy."

She pointed to one of the hitchracks and Greg nodded. She moved away without word or smile and Greg watched after her. She walked with a fast step but there was also a flowing grace, a set to slim figure that he admired. Finally he smiled quizzically and looked toward the bank. Maybe Moyers might work out to be as good as Unger as peacemaker. If a stubborn spitfire like Amanda . . .

He remembered. Cal waited for him. He swung on his heel and hurried to the cafe hitchrack where they had left the horses. Cal ambled out of the cafe door as Greg came up. "Looks like she didn't shoot you. What'd she do to Moyers?"

"Listened." His searching eyes found a saloon a short way down the street. "Let's have a drink, Cal, and then you go on out to the ranch. I'll be along later."

"The drink is fine. But, what kind of trouble you planning on now?"

"Nothing. I'm riding out later with her. She asked me if I would."

"It ain't you planning trouble. It's her. You'll need that drink and so will I."

XVII

━━━━◆━━━━

Amanda met Greg before the store with a small, almost chillingly formal smile. She avoided his hand to climb into the buggy and wheeled it out onto the square, leaving Greg to swing in the saddle and follow after.

She did not so much as glance at him as they worked their way out of the square. The houses of the town thinned and finally dropped completely behind them. Greg held the pace but wondered what the reason for her invitation might be. A mile passed before Amanda slowed the pace of the gray drawing the buggy.

She had folded the top back and afternoon sun made little blue glints in her black hair. Greg vividly remembered how she had looked the day he had driven the ambushers off. Now, the anger was gone and she looked pensively ahead down the road. She brushed a lock of hair off her cheek and her little frown deepened.

She beckoned Greg closer as he rode along beside the buggy. "Do you think Moyers will really be fair?"

"I got a real solid hunch he will. First I've met him, of course, but he looks no fool."

"But he worked for Bar Y."

"That again."

"Yes, that again. None of us can help bringing it up after all that's happened. But . . ."

She fell silent and studied the road again. Greg finally asked, "But?"

She made an impatient, puzzled shrug. "He made me look at things different. Same facts, same shooting and such but—"

"There could be other answers?"

"Something like that. Do you think Vale Edwards told the truth at my place?"

"I surely think so, at least as far as he knows. He took Yates' word for a lot of things. After we left your meeting, Yates was called up and Edwards sure threw questions. You heard Moyers say he'd been digging around at Bar Y, too."

Amanda considered the statement. "I didn't know about all that."

"Might've asked me, if not Edwards."

She looked embarrassed and trapped, but nodded. "I might. But it looked like you and Bar Y were working together."

"Like Stern said? I got to be for or against, nothing else?"

"Something like that." She suddenly looked up with a warm appeal for understanding. "Greg, have we seen everything wrong? Remember when we first met. I knew those bushwhackers were Bar Y. I knew everything else tied in with Yates and Bar Y. Now—well, Moyers makes me wonder."

"Glory be! If the rest of your friends do a little wondering and head scratching, things might clear up. That is, if Moyers is given the time he needs."

"But Bart Yates must be behind this if Edwards isn't," she protested.

"I've tallied him," Greg admitted. "But not hard and firm. Even with him there could be other answers. Maybe Bar Y is being hit like you are. He said as much to Edwards."

"Who'd do that?"

"I'd say someone who gains no matter who wins in a range war. Make that part of all our head scratching along with Moyers."

Far ahead, the Tumbling T road joined the main one. Amanda picked up the reins, let them fall again and held to the slow pace. She studied Greg, slowly flushed and forced her words. "Was I awful—with Diana Edwards?"

He grinned and her flush deepened. "Things sort of exploded in a hurry. It happens when tempers run high. Remember Stern even pulled a gun on me and grabbed Edwards. You did no more than him."

"But it didn't help at all, I can see that. I suppose she was mad at you afterward."

"Yes, for what it matters."

"But—I see," she said in a changed tone.

They had come now to Greg's road and Amanda stopped the buggy. She sat, reins held in folded hands on her lap. Greg said, "I could see you on to Rocking Chair?"

She started out of her thoughts. "Oh, no. There's no need. I'm so near home now."

Greg held the impatient bay in and it made little prancing steps. "I have to ask what you figure on doing."

She passed her hand across her cheek in a distracted gesture. "Fight, Greg. Oh, not the way you think! Dad swears Bart Yates shot him. Hal Stern swears Bar Y killed Sam. They've all heard about the rifled beef and I've sworn Bar Y did that. All but Hoskins have been for taking up guns. Now—"

"Hold 'em off?"

"If I can." She looked up. "You know what? I've been as

160

fire-eating as the rest, maybe more. How am I going to change my tune now?"

"Don't. Just argue patience. Hoskins will back you."

"I suppose so. Greg, do you think this thing will work out? I mean, Moyers will find who and what's behind it and we won't be hating one another?"

"Maybe. Worth a chance."

"You saw that from the beginning, Greg. We didn't. Lord! how much we'll have to repay for all the hard words, suspicion and—I confess for me—even close to hate at times. How can we?"

Greg answered uncomfortably. "You're giving me too much credit. I just wanted to save my ranch and my money. What's so all-fired grand about that?"

"Just more reason and sense than we've had. More trust in the law, maybe, less suspicion." She suddenly held her hand up to him. "Greg, forgive me?"

"Why—why . . ."

He suddenly saw her as she had been that day at the fence. Same soft eyes, and slightly parted lips, same vibrant body. But he knew a difference, at least in the way he sensed her. No use here of feminine weapons to win him over. Just darkly beautiful woman, honest enough to face a mistake and openly acknowledge an error.

He bent down and took her hand. Her fingers wrapped about his, warm and pleading. He searched her face, bent lower and her head lifted, eyes growing deep.

"Why, there's nothing to forgive. Maybe, when this is over, you'll have to forgive me. I could be all-fired wrong. Bar Y might—"

"It doesn't matter about Bar Y!" she said sharply. "It's the way we—I—wanted to be lawman, jury and judge. You knew better. That's what I'm saying."

He clung to her hand a moment longer and then released it, straightened in the saddle. He said with a stiffness he couldn't keep out of his voice, "Main thing is, we keep in touch. Maybe I could ride over . . . ?"

She smiled. "I'll expect you. Any time."

She slapped the reins on the gray rump of the horse and the buggy rolled away down the road. Greg held in the bay. The black vehicle grew steadily smaller as distance lengthened and then disappeared around a far curve of the road. The bay made an impatient move to start toward home but Greg tight-checked the bit, unaware of it.

The faint lift of dust from buggy wheels slowly dissipated. Greg smoothed fingers thoughtfully along his jaw. What a strange mixture of qualities in Amanda Zane! A fighter, as when he had first seen her, exchanging bullet for bullet. A capable rancher, as he had later learned, running Rocking Chair when her father could no longer handle it. Organizer—bringing all the small ranches into a coherent, purposeful group. And yet, with all these masculine abilities, a woman a man would long remember and a woman a man could want. A loyalty in her, instinctive and sure—to friends, to beliefs and to responsibilities.

Today he had discovered yet another rare quality, that of facing facts and acknowledging error, or at least its possibility. Greg suddenly wondered if Hal Stern would accuse Amanda of being a turncoat.

Greg made a grimace, and his hand relaxed on the reins. The bay, sensing permission, turned to the ranch road and with toss of head moved off toward corral, stable and feed.

Cal waited in the kitchen doorway when Greg came in from the stable. He stepped aside, asking, "How mad did she get at you?"

"None."

"Then you sure must've joined up with her and the others! No other way she'd see it."

"Wrong. She just might join up with us."

Cal stopped short on his way to the range and the cook-

162

ing pots. "You must've done a lot of roping and hog-tying. 'Manda Zane ain't one to back down to nobody."

"She didn't, just looked at things differently."

Cal went to the range, banged noisily as he lifted stove lids and stoked the fire. He finally spoke drily over his shoulder. "Beats me how a stranger like you can swing such a wide loop and make so many changes."

Two days later, Moyers stopped by. The sheriff accepted coffee in the sun-dappled kitchen. "Me'n Hal Stern have been going over and over his story about Sam's killing. He sort of changes things here and there—between what he told Mary Ralls and me—and now there's more."

"Such as?"

"I made him go to Bar Y. He couldn't find the man he claimed to see in the crew over there. We rode out to where Sam was killed and I made Stern show me where he was, and Sam—and where he met the stranger. Hal's getting uncertain in the little details."

"What do you think now?"

"Hard to say, except Hal's nervous and mad. Bart Yates didn't look any too happy, either, when Vale had him round up the whole crew for Stern to look over. Oh, and I dropped in at Rocking Chair. Wes Zane still sticks to the story it was Yates shot him."

"And Amanda?"

"Believes her father one way, uncertain another. But she and Hoskins have the rest waiting to see what'll happen instead of breathing fire and bullets like they were. It comes from you bringing her around to see me."

Moyers left and Tumbling T settled into routine work. Yet both Greg and Cal did not trust the peaceful succession of the days. They caught themselves looking with tense expectancy toward the horizon that bound the ranch. They looked forward to Saturday in Redman, where they might learn of developments.

The night before, Greg made a list of needed supplies to be bought in town then he and Cal turned into bed in their separate rooms. Greg fell asleep almost instantly and he had no idea what time it was when his eyes snapped open.

He sat upright in bed, the darkness of the room pressing about him. He wondered what had caused the shock of nerves that had awakened him. He heard a stirring in the hall and he swung back the covers. He groped for the lamp when Cal's low voice sounded from the doorway.

"Greg? Awake? Don't strike a light."

"What's wrong?"

"Something in the barn. Horses restless out there."

"I'll get dressed."

He found the chair holding his trousers and shirt, and heard the receding stir of Cal's steps in the hallway. Greg hurried into clothing, felt about for boots beside the bed. He heard a faint creak of the kitchen door and called softly, "Cal! Wait for me! Might be—!"

He cursed, knowing that Cal had gone out into the yard. He found his boots, worked into them. He crossed the room to the bureau and his fingers struck leather and loops of his gunbelt. He swung it around his waist and buckled it as he moved to the dark kitchen.

He pushed open the door, stepped out and stood with senses probing the night. He heard a muffled thump from the barn, horses stirring. Eyes adjusted to the night yard, he saw a faint movement, knew Cal ghosted forward to the barn. Greg stepped away from the house.

Cal faded into the darkness ahead, his shadow blending with that of the barn. Suddenly a low voice called, "Corwin? That you?"

"Who's that?" Cal called.

"Get in here! They'll be sneaking up any minute and you won't have a chance."

164

"Who's sneaking?"

Greg moved cautiously just a few yards behind the old man. He could see the black maw of the open barn door, Cal's indistinct figure. Greg held his Colt with hammer dogged back. He heard Cal's swift steps to the barn and he called urgently, "Wait! Don't know who it—"

Roar of a gun and a lance of orange-red flame from the barn door cut him off. He saw Cal spin half around, making a strange grunting sound. A shadow moved swiftly out of the door, ghosting along the front of the barn to the corner. Greg yelled, "Hold it!" as his gun swung onto the shadow.

His answer came. Another roar, lance of flame and the slapping whine of a bullet beside his ear. Greg flinched away but swung the Colt muzzle, following the vanishing figure as he pulled the trigger. Roar of gun partially drowned a scream. Greg heard a threshing low on the ground over by the corner of the barn.

He swung around to find Cal. The old man grunted, "Nicked, that's all. Make sure of that killer. He could shoot again."

Greg swung back. He still heard movement and he advanced cautiously, Colt ready to fire. Within a few steps he made out the shadowy shape lying at the corner. He heard a groan. Greg edged to the man, lined gun on him and bent down. The man lay with his head tossing back and forth and his torso heaving as though he tried to lift himself by his shoulder blades. Greg caught a dull gleam a few feet away and recognized a gun.

Certain now, Greg hastily holstered his gun, fished out matches and struck one with a flick of thumbnail. The glare revealed Hal Stern's pain racked face. Dark, haunted eyes fixed on Greg and the tossing head froze as the eyes widened. "Corwin! I shot you—"

"Cal Weber—not me."

The head tossed again. "Don't matter. Need a doctor bad.

165

Took the slug . . . my back. Chest empty—smashed up . . . I'm scared!"

Greg slowly moved Stern, lifting gently. Striking another match, he saw the pool of dark blood under Stern and he gently lowered him. Stern choked, "Get a doctor!"

"I—no use, Hal."

The head froze again and the eyes rested in rounded horror on Greg. The torso strained but Greg, with a firm, easy pressure, stopped the attempt. "You'll just kill yourself sooner, Hal."

"No! No!" A gulp of breath and then a catching whisper. "How long?"

"I don't know. I'd guess—minutes."

"You killed me!" There was the full force of a scream in the weakening voice. "Shot me in the back!"

"Like you did Sam Ralls?"

"You knew. All the time you knew. I could tell that day you rode out . . . You sent Moyers. You told him."

"I didn't know anything, Hal. Guessed, maybe, but so did Moyers. The swale and tree and bushes didn't fit your story. Besides, you told Mary Ralls you were with him *all* the time. No, I just guessed."

The head moved more slowly from side to side and Stern's eyes grew heavy. He murmured, "Knew—all the time. Knew too much. You could tell—and . . . I tried—"

"To shut me up?" Stern didn't answer and Greg asked sharply, "Why did you kill Sam?"

"He said . . . easy the way I did it. Just pulled my gun . . . maybe a foot away, or less . . . pull the trigger . . ."

"Why? Who's 'He'?"

"Him! I'd run Anchor, he said, if Ralls was . . . Manage it until . . . after things blow over . . ."

The voice faded away and Stern's body stiffened and then fell into the complete slackness of death. Greg struck his

166

fourth match, let it burn down and then swung around, still at a crouch. "Cal?"

"Bullet gored my leg like a bull's horn but nothing broken. Just bleeding like a stuck pig."

Greg hurried to the old man, almost falling over him in the darkness. Cal now sat up and when Greg struck another match, he saw he had shrugged out of his shirt ripped off a sleeve and had it tightly bound about his left leg above the knee. The cloth was badly stained.

"Tighten it up!" Greg snapped. "I'll get a stick."

He lunged into the barn, found the lantern hanging just inside the door and lit it. He snatched up a small piece of wood lying on the floor. In another moment, he knelt beside Cal, ripping out the other shirt sleeve. He snatched off the soaked cloth, slapped the new on, snap-tied it about the stick and twisted. The crude tourniquet worked and the bleeding slowed, stopped. Greg put the old puncher's hand to the stick.

"Hold the pressure. You need a sawbones. I'll hitch up the buckboard."

"Ain't no need—"

"Hush! I'll feel better. And I want to get Stern to Redman and the sheriff."

"I heard him. Every word. Why'd Stern shoot Ralls?"

"If you heard, you know."

"Sure, ain't thinking clear. But who promised he could run Anchor?"

"If any of us knew that . . . No time now. Keep still and hold that twist tight."

Greg hurried to the barn and by lantern light hitched the team to the buckboard. He rolled out and helped Cal to his feet and, with a few hopping steps, to the buckboard. The awkward, straining movements caused the tourniquet to slip and blood flowed. As soon as Cal had stretched out, Greg applied the twisting pressure and the blood stopped.

Then Greg, carrying the lantern, went to Stern. He started as he held the lantern low. In death, the malignant expression that had so surprised him had settled permanently on Stern's features. Greg went through the man's pockets. There were all the usual things a puncher would carry, nothing more. Greg replaced the knife, coins and soiled handkerchief and started to lift the man. He felt something thick around the waist. Greg ripped down the trousers to disclose a new money belt. Within it, Greg found bright gold coins. Thirty twenty-dollar pieces—six hundred dollars.

Greg studied the golden glint in the lantern's glow and then replaced them, swung money belt over his shoulder. He dragged the body to the buckboard and, with a series of heaves, Hal Stern finally fell beside Cal Weber, who edged away.

Greg snuffed out the lantern, jumped up into the seat and snapped reins over the team. They rolled out of Tumbling T in the dark night toward Redman. Cal cursed softly now and then. Greg puzzled about "he" who gave promises and gold coins.

XVIII

As Greg rolled into Redman, every house sat squat and dark, and the buckboard echoed and rattled. When he entered the square, he saw only fans of light from two saloons.

Greg turned in at Doc Robbins' office. It, too, was dark but Greg kept pounding on the door until it jerked open and Doc peered out, shirt tail hanging out over hastily donned pants. "Who's sick?"

"Shot. Cal Weber. I think it's a flesh wound but I brought him in. Slug's still in his leg."

Doc looked beyond at the shadowy buckboard. "Can he walk? . . . Good, then help him in while I strike a light and get things ready."

By the time Greg had helped Cal out and supported him across the walk, lamplight glowed from the windows and Robbins lunged out to help. He stopped short, peering at the buckboard, and then at Cal. "Two? I thought there was just one."

"That one's dead. It's Hal Stern. I shot him after he hit Cal. I'm taking him to the sheriff."

Robbins whistled softly. "You just shot yourself into a

whole passel of trouble, friend. But right now, we've got this one to look over."

The wound, as lamplight revealed, had bled some more but the tourniquet had proved effective. Doc Robbins examined the wound. "Slug's there, all right. So, out she has to come. I'll use chloroform, Cal. You won't feel a thing."

Greg stood by to help but Cal slept through the probing and recovery of the slug. Robbins started to clean the wound preparatory to bandaging it. "You can't do any good here, Corwin. Better get over to the Sheriff."

"Cal can stay here the rest of the night?"

"I'd like it that way. Maybe Moyers will want to talk to him come daylight."

Greg hurried out, crossed the square to the courthouse and a few moments later emerged with Moyers at his heel. The lawman peered at Stern's face, ghostly in the starlight. Moyers looked around the square, deserted except for a few horses at a distant saloon hitchrack. "Best get Hal out of sight for the time being. I've got all empty cells tonight, thank God. Time enough for the undertaker come morning, or even the next day."

Moyers went ahead to open doors as Greg swung the team around. They lifted the stiffening body and carried it inside, grunted their way to a cell and placed it on the floor. Moyers examined the dead man by lamplight, square face tight with a new worry. He arose. "Let's get to the office."

In the office, Moyers' voice became flat and expressionless as he threw questions, went back over the story several times. Greg placed Stern's money belt on the desk and Moyers counted the gold coins. He gave Greg a piercing, underbrow look. "Weber's over at Robbins' office?"

"That's right, but sound asleep." Greg explained the chloroform. "Doc's holding him until you ask all the questions you want."

170

"I will. And you stay in town. The hotel's the other side of the courthouse." Moyers touched the coins. "What do you figure?"

"Brand new. More'n a puncher or a foreman would carry around. He'd keep them cached in the bunkhouse unless . . ."

"What?"

"He couldn't explain them and was afraid they'd be turned up somehow."

"Who do you figure 'he' is?"

Greg threw his hands wide. "I figured you might have an idea."

Moyers swept the coins back into the money belt, took it to a small safe. He closed the door, twirled the knob and returned to his desk. "Six hundred dollars—brand, mint new. Maybe, last time he was in town, he traded old money in."

"When was he in town?"

"Night before this. Surprised me, too. I told you I was working his story over and getting changes. Little changes, but a straight, true story don't need even little ones. Hal wandered along the square from saloon to saloon. He ran into Yates—"

"Yates?"

"In town on Bar Y business. But, hell, Stern ran into Unger and I know damn' well the banker . . ."

His voice faded off and Greg said, "Brand, mint new. Had Stern been at the bank?"

"Not that I know of."

"Worth thinking about. Yates—him and Unger friendly?"

"Yates reps Bar Y and they do business with the bank. Yates is always in and out. For that matter, Vale himself visits Unger. I know. I worked for Bar Y once."

"You were not part of the new crew, were you? . . . I thought not. How were they hired?"

"Bar Y troubles started and Yates told Edwards he needed

171

a tough crew to meet a tough fight. So Edwards told Yates to do as he saw fit."

"But just how did Yates hire 'em?"

"I reckon he wrote letters to men he knew. I know they had their expenses paid getting here. He arranged it with Unger to send the money and charge Bar Y's account at the bank. They'd come in by ones and twos, go to the bank and Unger'd send them on to Bar Y."

"Unger keeps coming up."

"Forget it. I remember he told me—and a dozen others —he didn't want gunhawks coming into Sioux Valley. But Bar Y ordered and paid for it, so what could he do?

Greg yawned and stood up. "Maybe both of us had better sleep on it. I'll be at the hotel when you want me come morning."

Greg drove to the livery stable and then walked to the hotel through the night-dark square. He thought of Cal at the doctor's office, Stern dead in the courthouse cell, of Mary Ralls, Amanda Zane, Bart Yates and Diana, of Unger and fat, troubled Hoskins—trying to fit them into a pattern that explained the ugly current sweeping Sioux Valley.

He had not succeeded by the time he checked in, found his room and dropped into bed. After a few moments restless tossing, he dropped off into a sound sleep.

His eyes snapped open to early morning sunshine and a cool breeze blowing through the window. He swung his legs out of bed, fought away the last remnants of sleep, and stepped to the window. He could see the courthouse, white and bright in clear sunshine, dominating the square. Beyond, he saw the brick of the bank and recalled the only time he had been inside the building.

Frederick Unger, trusted by all in Sioux Valley and one who could certainly have no axe to grind, would make the perfect peacemaker. Yet he had wanted to think over something that stood up as plain and factual as the courthouse building itself. Greg's mind chewed on that and then, aware the morning moved on, he hastily dressed.

At the doctor's office, Cal complained, "What's to check on this damn' leg? The slug's out and nothing's busted or anything."

Greg mollified, "Maybe by tonight or tomorrow we'll get you back to the ranch. Besides, Moyers wants to talk to you about what happened."

Robbins came in and Cal scowled at his professional cheerfulness. Greg waited as the wound was checked, cleaned and rebandaged. The Sheriff came as Robbins finished and the lawman went over the events of the night before in a series of sharp questions that Cal answered. Moyers repeated some of the questions, wording them differently and then, at last, eased back in his chair.

Robbins, who had remained, asked in awed surprise, "Stern shot his own boss?"

Moyers answered grimly, "I'd begun to suspect it myself. Now—what Cal heard—we know. Doc, breathe one word of what you've heard and you'll live in one of my cells."

"What about Stern? You can't keep his body hidden."

"I don't figure on it. But I'm not saying who shot him or why, or say anything about him killing Sam."

"Folks'll think all sorts of things and blame everyone in sight. It'll be Bar Y did it—or some hotheaded little rancher. Things get twisted bad enough with facts but even worse without. The whole valley will explode."

Moyers looked at Greg as though asking advice. Greg spoke to Robbins. "Stern did the killing because someone paid him to do it—in cash and with some kind of promises. That man ought to worry enough to show his hand."

Robbins looked from man to man and then nodded. "You're taking a big gamble. The gravediggers and I could be mighty busy in a week. But I'll go along."

Moyers slapped his hands on his knees and arose, giving

Greg a small signal. Outside, Moyers turned a troubled gaze on him. "Doc's right. I've been thinking—Amanda Zane, can you talk her into holding her people still for a few days?"

"I can try. Tell her why?"

"No more'n we're on a fresh trail and don't want some damn' fool act to erase it. Will that do?"

"For a time. You figure like I do, I'll bet. Stern's friend ain't one of the small ranchers."

"Who would you guess?"

"Like you, one of three. What are you going to do?"

"Give Stern to the undertaker and then ride out to Bar Y. And you?"

"Have something to eat, do some thinking and watch what happens around town when they learn about Stern."

"Let me know when I get back."

Moyers walked off and Greg went to a cafe down the street.

Just as Greg finished his coffee, a man rushed in with news Hal Stern had been shot. There was an immediate hubbub, questions thrown and speculations circulating. Some in the cafe accused Bar Y's owner, foreman or one of its crew. Others guessed that an Anchor neighbor had finished a job started with Sam Ralls. Everyone agreed that Sioux Valley guns would blaze within less than a week.

Greg returned to his hotel. He sat on the deep verandah, watching the life of the square as his mind worried at the knot of the gold coins, the promise and "he." He arrived at one satisfying conclusion—there had been a third party in this trouble, that is if he had not read Vale Edwards wrong.

Just before noon, Greg wandered to the Rancher's Rest. Lafferty greeted him and poured out the news of Stern's killing and the river of speculations let loose because of it. Greg listened until the man ran out of speech, then he went to a table and laid out a solitaire game.

Unger came in, saw Greg and dropped into a chair, signaled Lafferty to bring bottle and glasses. Greg smiled answer to his greeting. Unger's gaunt, saturnine face seemed subtly more angular.

When Lafferty had departed, Unger filled the two shot glasses, pushed one to Greg, lifted his own. "To a man who can think better than I can—you."

"That's a hell of a toast! Why?"

"The other day—when you came to the bank. Somehow, you saw what was coming and a way out of it. I didn't see how I might have stopped it. Now I do. So . . . to your clear thinking."

"I take the drink but not the credit. How could any of us know?"

"About Hal Stern! You've heard, of course? Who could have done it?"

Unger made guesses. Greg, having pushed the cards aside, listened. He found himself thinking back to the beginning of this business as he had known it. He saw it as an involved secret game in which the apparent actors were moved by a force even they might not be aware of. That force—what or who? "He?" As though Greg had somehow picked up a thread, unrecognized at first, he discovered unrelated events began to make sense and form a pattern. The conviction grew and, with it, the knowledge that he had to gamble to prove it. He fought the impulse, as he first thought it to be, and then realized it was more an inner, intuitive knowledge.

He cut in on Unger. "Still want to buy Tumbling T?"

Unger's mouth hung open, snapped shut. His eyes hooded and an instant later opened wide in sorrow. "Not now. Not at any price. I'm pulling in horns until I see what happens."

"Until the guns stop? It figures. Do you reckon it'll ruin the Valley? Say, Bar Y?"

"Ruin? Maybe . . . more like change. Bar Y? It won't sur-

175

prise me they'll have to use that fighting crew Yates hired. The others—Hoskins, Zanes, and such—will blame 'em for Stern, like they have for everything else. I'm surprised it hasn't come to a head by now."

Greg kept his eyes on his fingers. "Gun power at Bar Y, more 'n the others. A man might need that."

"You're trying to say something, Greg?"

"I need a friend who can smooth things over with Bart Yates. It was all a mistake, anyhow, that fight we had. Could you do it? Maybe this could make up for that other mistake you made."

Unger leaned elbows on the table. "I do business with Bart. He listens to me. But what do you want with him?"

"I'm going to need his guns. Can I trust you to help and keep your mouth shut?"

"A banker learns that trick. I told you once before, I like you. Try me."

Greg poured a drink for himself, tossed it down, using the opportunity to judge Unger's reaction. The man sat tense. Greg lowered the glass. "All right, I'll tell you. I killed Stern."

Unger flinched. His surprise was real and so, Greg sensed, was his consternation. "You! But why?"

"He figured I'd told Moyers he'd killed Sam Ralls. And he had. He confessed."

"Confessed? Did he say why?"

"Someone paid him to. He had brand new gold coins in a money belt I found on him. Stern said someone promised him he'd run Anchor."

Unger dropped back in his chair. He took a deep breath and the mantle of his usual assurance fell on him again. "This is amazing, Greg."

"If it gets out I shot Stern before me or Moyers find the gent behind him, the Zanes and the rest will come gunning for me. So I need Bar Y help and that means Yates. But he needn't know the rest of it. Can you persuade him that I want to throw in on his side?"

"I—maybe, maybe. But have you any idea who was behind Stern?"

"Idea, yes. But I need time to prove it."

Unger made a distressed gesture. "I'll see Bart."

"Tell him to forget the fight. It's over and done so far as I'm concerned. I'll help him if he'll help me."

Unger arose, adjusted his coat and, with the gesture, recovered his balance. He placed a hand on Greg's shoulder. "Don't worry, I'll not miss this chance to help. If Bart wants to see you, will you be in town?"

Greg thought quickly. "Just today but out at the ranch from tomorrow on. Maybe Bart had best see me then—that is if you can—"

"Oh, I will! I'll get right out to Bar Y. And you can depend on me to keep my mouth shut."

"Just long enough I can find the jasper behind Stern."

"Does Moyers know about all this?"

"Sure, except what I've been able to figure out."

"Who?"

"No names—because it's not proof. I aim to get that— maybe today—anyhow by the end of the week."

"I'm sure you will. But don't worry about anything."

He squeezed Greg's shoulder again and hurried out. Greg sat quite still but his mind swung in a wild turmoil. He could imagine Moyers' anger if he knew Unger had been told the full facts. But Greg knew he had acted correctly—or at least logic, pointing in only one direction, backed his gamble.

Greg looked at the clock. Moyers should be back in town early afternoon. No matter when Unger talked to Yates— and Greg was as certain of that conference as he was of his breathing—there would be time to set the stage for the final showdown at Tumbling T. That would come inevitably now.

177

Greg swept up the scattered cards and dealt another solitaire layout. There would be little else to do until Moyers returned. Greg played slowly. Once, as he thought of what he planned, he felt a cold shiver down his back.

He hastily dropped the black king on the red ace.

XIX

———◆———

Facing Moyers' initial wrath over Greg's telling the whole story to Unger had not been pleasant. But gradually the lawman had come to Greg's logical conclusion. He had told Greg to stay in the office and he left, to return in ten minutes to say he had seen Unger ride off.

"To Bar Y and Yates. If you're wrong, you'll feel like a fool, Corwin. But you could also be dead right with a dozen slugs in your brisket."

"That's where I need you—and Amanda Zane."

So the next morning, he ordered Cal, over angry protests, to stay in town for another day. Then Greg waited for the bank to open. He soon found himself in Unger's office. The banker closed the door, turned and said, "It took some doing, but Bart thinks he might go along—after he talks to you."

"Tonight?"

"At your place. Might be late. Bar Y's busy these days."

"Anytime," Greg said with mock relief. "How about Edwards? He coming along, too?"

"I said nothing to him. Didn't think you wanted any more than Bart and me to know about this business."

"That's right. I kind of worried."

Greg thanked Unger, left the bank and soon rode out on the buckboard. He circled to the far side of the courthouse, out of sight of the bank, and hurried to the sheriff's office. "Well, part of it's working. I'll meet you a mile out on the south road."

Greg rattled out of Redman, heading south toward Tumbling T. He glanced back now and then through the dustcloud his buckboard raised along the road. No one followed so far as he could determine. A mile or so out, he pulled in under the shade of a tree and set himself to wait.

In an hour Sheriff Moyers pulled into the shade beside the buckboard and slouched in the saddle as he squinted back down the road. He asked, "Now what? Just you and me against a dozen or so guns?"

"Rocking Chair first. I think we can even the odds."

Moyers face lighted. "Amanda should fair jump at this chance. She's been waiting long enough. Let's ride."

Just before noon, the two men rode into Rocking Chair yard. Wes Zane sat under the trees where the fighting conference had been held. Amanda Zane appeared in the ranch house doorway as Greg and Moyers rode up and dismounted. She waited at the edge of the porch, puzzled and frowning.

Greg said, "We come for your help. The sheriff's ready to make his move and arrest and he needs a posse. Would your hands and your friends like to pitch in?"

"What?"

Her voice lifted in a cry of delighted amazement. Out under the trees, Wes turned his chair and called, "What's breaking loose now, 'Manda?"

She hurried with them to the waiting man. Amanda hastily pulled up other chairs and Greg told what had happened, starting with Hal Sterns' attempt to kill him.

"But we heard Bar Y killed Hal," Amanda broke in. "Sheriff, we figured you'd—well, thrown in with your old outfit. Hoskins and the others will be in this afternoon to decide what to do."

Greg laughed. "Couldn't be better. But wait until we line the rest of it out and you'll see why."

He brought up all the events that pointed in just one direction. Wes Zane pounded a fist on his chair arm. "I knew I had the right man tallied! I knew it! It's him."

Amanda said, "And we were right all the time about Bar Y. Vale Edwards just sat back and saw to it thing's happened through Bart Yates. He had you fooled, Greg."

Greg threw a glance at Moyers, who shook his head. Greg smiled crookedly. "Main thing is, I told you I'd throw in when there was proof against someone and when the law made your friends a posse instead of a bunch of raiders. You'll deputize them, Moyers?"

"Everyone that shows up and wants to ride."

Amanda jumped up. "This will be the end, won't it? The very end! We can all live in peace."

"Once it's over," Greg agreed. "I'd best get home and be ready for our visitors. They might come earlier than I figure. Sheriff, you know where to meet me? Amanda, we'll let you know what happens."

"Thanks for that. I'll look for you."

Greg left the group, swung the buckboard around and drove off. He looked back to see Moyers and Amanda in a deep discussion under the trees and then he gave his full attention to the road ahead.

Tumbling T looked and felt empty but for all he knew, he was watched from the distant hillocks. He drove to the barn, unhitched the buckboard and walked to the house.

The day slowly waned. Now and then Greg, roaming from kitchen to parlor, studied the road and the surrounding hills. No one appeared, nothing stirred. Greg oiled, cleaned and reloaded his rifle and Colt. He shoved extra cartridges into his pockets and then resumed the difficult task of waiting and watching.

Near sundown, he cooked a supper of sorts. He knew that lifting smoke from the chimney above the house would signal his presence. He ate, seated near the window, watching the slow gather of dusk. He began to feel a sense of time pressing close.

He lit the lamp, knowing the glow through the window would make a golden spot in the gathering dark. He carried it to the bedroom, pulled down the blind. Then he grabbed up rifle and went outside.

Stars showed clear and Greg knew he could not be seen beyond a few yards. He ghosted to the stable, worked silently and quickly saddling the bay. He mounted and moved cautiously out of the yard. A dim peaceful glow came from the bedroom, the buildings seemed to sleep in darkness. Beyond, the land had faded away. Satisfied, Greg cut obliquely away from the road.

A hundred or so yards out he came on the darker line of trees and bushes. Moyers' voice made a soft call in the night. "Corwin? All right?"

Greg drifted into the shadow of the trees. He saw mounted shapes all about him, faces indistinct in the darkness. Moyers loomed close and Greg said, "So far we're lucky."

"What's your plan?"

"I figure whoever comes, alone or with gunhawks, will hail the house first. They'll come in from the north and they'll go back that way once it's over."

"So we cut 'em off," Moyers answered. Another figure came up, small and slight, big hat brim cutting off even the gray shape that marked a face. Moyers continued, "But we'll leave a few down here in case they cut away in this direction."

"That'll do it."

182

Moyers turned to the newcomer. "This will be the safest place. So I'll leave you with Hoskins and three-four others, Amanda."

Greg gasped, "Amanda!"

"Couldn't keep her from coming. Maybe you can talk her into going home or dropping 'way back where she won't be hurt."

The sheriff drifted off to pass low orders. Greg leaned forward in the saddle. She swept off her big hat and he saw the delicate shape of her face. He exploded, though his voice remained low, "Of all the crazy things! Why did you have to come? This is no place for a woman!"

"It is for this woman, Greg Corwin. Don't try to order me away. Everyone's tried it this afternoon but here I am. Here I stay and I intend to take a hand."

"But can't you see—"

"I've seen my cattle killed and fences cut. I've seen my father shot and lucky to be alive, though he's maybe crippled for life. Sam Ralls killed by a man he trusted, and that man bought by Bar Y."

"Sure, but—"

"Who has worked hardest to get someone to stand up and fight? Do you think I'm going to sit home, just because I'm a woman, and let others finish what I've been hellbent bound to do from the beginning? Greg Corwin, you just don't know Amanda Zane!"

After a moment, Greg said, "I guess I don't, but I'm beginning to. Anyhow, you'll stay with the bunch here."

She replaced her hat and the two sat silent, side by side, hearing the slight stir of men around them. Greg touched Colt in holster and ran his fingers over the rifle stock in its scabbard. Amanda's horse tossed its head and she spoke a quiet, firm word.

He marveled, sensing the depths of her loyalties and determination. She had an inner, fiery strength, not wholly

183

a blind force, as he knew from the way she had conceded Moyers' reasons for moving slowly. She had not, nor would not, give friendship and loyalty on impulse, but once given a man could depend on it. She would fight to the frazzled end for what or whoever she believed in.

Her low voice broke the silence, "Greg?"

"Yes?"

"Tonight—your ranch out there. What will happen to it?"

"I don't know."

"We'll see nothing does," she said flatly and fell silent again.

He looked out on darkness toward the buildings that he could not see. The shadowy men and horses about him had edge rather than blur. His ears keened for sound out beyond the trees.

His mind picked up strange thoughts and new relationships. Here he sat among men almost strangers, waiting for what might prove to be a whirlwind, because of a snow storm and a card game. What had happened to the Texan whose poker status Greg had destroyed?

Mary Ralls—what did she do now? Sit alone in a dark house, mourning a dead husband and the treachery that had snatched him away? Had someone told her yet about Stern? What would she do?

Diana Edwards, perhaps sleeping secure in a big ranch—what would the morning bring to her? Would it matter about Bart Yates? Greg wondered if Diana, trading situation with Amanda, would be sitting a horse in the night, calmly expecting a gun battle? Or would she stay home and wait, in the accepted way of women?

She would wait, he decided. She moved with circumstances, shaping only the moment to her secret plans. She was not one to stand up against opposition. Not that she was weak or did not have spark and spirit, but that she—

"Listen!" Amanda hissed.

184

Greg peered into the night, ears keened. He heard nothing but the sigh of a small wind that had sprung up. At this distance, the glow of light behind the bedroom blind resembled a dim, golden star that had slipped from its position in the dark sky.

Then, under and blending with the wind, a far-off whisper of movement. A stir rippled down the line. A moment later, the whisper came, "Time to move with Moyers."

Greg impulsively groped for Amanda's hand and found it. He felt the swift, warm pressure of her fingers and he said, "Stay right here. Keep yourself safe."

"Of course, Greg, of course!"

He drifted away, aware of the warmth of her voice. He came to Moyers in the group of slow moving riders. The sheriff led the way out beyond the far end of the trees, made a wide loop that would bring them in position between the ranch buildings and the hills to the north.

Off to the left, the night seemed undisturbed but Greg knew threat drifted and stirred out there. Moyers leaned toward him. "I sent one of Hoskins' riders out as scout. He heard them drifting in. He said it sounded like at least a dozen riders, maybe more."

"The whole crew!"

"Every gunslinger Yates has on the payroll. You've called the shots, Corwin."

"All but the last and let's hope . . ."

His whisper drifted off. Greg rode with hand close to his holster and ears attuned to the silent ranch. The lamp glow disappeared as they moved, far out, around the distant house.

Down that way, a voice broke the silence. "Corwin! Hey, Corwin! You wanted to see me?"

"Move in," Greg softly urged and Moyers passed along the order.

Now a shadowy line extended to either side, Moyers

looming to Greg's right. They drifted in toward the ranch, guns out of holsters, rifles held with fingers in trigger guards.

"Corwin!" the voice sounded near. "You coming out or do we come in?"

Barn and corral loomed ghostly just ahead and Moyers passed a whispered order that halted the line. The ranch house itself stood a darker shadow far ahead and Greg saw a shifting dark mass, marking horsemen.

A voice carried clearly. "Hell, Bart! Why wait? Blast him out and let's get back before the old man knows we're gone."

Greg, even as his muscles tightened, felt a surge of relief. Vale Edwards did not know of this nocturnal expedition. He was cleared, confirming Greg's logic.

"Move in?" Moyers whispered.

"No. So far, it's just a visit that I asked for."

"At near midnight with a dozen hardcases?"

"Give it a few minutes."

Moyers passed orders to stand tight. There came a sudden banging on a door. Time passed, each moment straining at the nerves. Greg heard muffled sounds from within the house and he had to restrain the impulse to rush forward.

Bart Yates' voice sounded loud. "Tex! Joe! He ain't here."

"Run out scared, Bart?"

"Maybe—or talking his damn' head off. Lot of good that'll do! Anyhow, fire the place. He won't have anything to come back to."

Steps echoed on the porch. Moyers said, "Move in. And watch yourselves."

Greg sank spurs and raced around the corral to the house. The roll of hoofs sounded like unexpected thunder and Greg heard a yell, saw a gunflash.

The night erupted and boiled. Renegades swung to saddle, some ran out of the house and lunged for their mounts. Greg and the others hit the group, splitting it wide. Men fell from saddles and gun thunder deafened the ears. A Colt spat fire almost in Greg's face but the slug whipped by his cheek. He fired and a figure toppled out and down into darkness.

Shadowy riders fanned away from the charge, the renegade band breaking up into splintered fragments that sought the night's safety. There was none for, beyond them, came triumphant yells and another charge as Hoskins' group took a hand. Greg hoped that Amanda stayed beneath the trees.

A gun flashed from his porch as Greg swung the bay about and his slug sent the fighter tumbling off the porch, gun firing uselessly into the ground. Now raiders, meeting the second group, came fleeing back, a pitiful few of them. Some tried to veer off. Others reined in, threw guns away and raised their hands, calling surrender.

It was over in a few more tumultuous moments. Suddenly all guns stopped though ears still roared until gradually the night sounds returned and a fading roll of hoofs as a few gunhawks escaped the net and fled. Greg yelled for light, dreading for Amanda.

Matches flared as she pushed through the crowd of riders. Greg, relieved, swung from the saddle, jumped into the house. He found a lamp, lit it. A glance told him the house had not been harmed. He raced outside, holding the lamp high.

In the middle of a rough circle of riders with drawn guns half a dozen men sat their horses, arms high, blinking against the lamp light that Greg held up to each face. Beyond the circle, Hoskins called, "We got four to bury!"

Greg half heard. Relief that Amanda sat alive and slender among the riders was shot through with need to see one face. He did not find Bart Yates. He recognized one sullen, stubbled face. "You," Greg snapped, "you and two friends tried to rifle down Amanda Zane."

"That ain't so."

"I drove you off and I had a good look at you."

187

Moyers pushed forward. "He'll see jail and a court then. Where's Yates?"

None of the gunhawks replied. Moyers settled in his saddle. "I'll hand it straight to you snakes. You know you've been part of a scheme to grab off the Valley. You've ambushed, burned and killed cattle. There's also murder to count for. Hal Stern worked for Yates, like the rest of you. You're all implicated."

"Now wait!" one protested.

"Like hell! You're going to jail, everyone of you. You know anyone who's part of a murder scheme hangs just as high as the one who did the actual killing. You got ten seconds to make up your minds to answer questions. If you don't, you'll hang for murder—every manjack."

He waited. Greg understood Moyers' tactic, for these men feared a hangrope more than they did a gun. Moyers broke the silence. "Who set you to ambush, burning and cattle killing?"

A stir and exchange of looks between the gunhawks. Each mistrusted the other, feared betrayal if he remained silent. One man surily answered, "Bart Yates hired us. He told us what to do."

"What do you know about Hal Stern?"

"Nothing," another spoke up. "But he met Bart lots of times. Bart said he was working for us and to leave him alone, no matter how ornery he acted toward Bar Y."

Amanda's voice crackled. "And he nearly persuaded us to go up against a gun crew!"

"Yes, ma'am. We'd been told to expect it."

"What do you know about Ralls' murder?"

"Nothing," an instant answer came. "None of us was anywhere near. Bart saw to that. But we heard about it and Bart said we'd have Anchor now."

Moyers asked, "Just Bart Yates? or someone behind him?"

188

A man spoke sullenly. "Can't answer that. From what Bart said, we knowed he had backing."

"Vale Edwards?" Amanda demanded.

"I don't know."

"But you'd guess him?" she insisted.

"How you want me to answer?"

"The truth!"

"I don't know."

Greg made an impatient sound. "Yates was here and he's gone. We're wasting time."

Moyers turned to Hoskins and indicated the captured men. "Keep 'em staked out until daylight. Then bring 'em to Redman. I'll meet you there." He turned to Greg. "Which way do we start looking for Yates?"

"Bar Y. He'd head there before he'd light out of the country—and that's all he can do after this round-up."

Moyers headed for his horse. Greg hurried after him, swung into the saddle while other men also mounted. Hoskins gave orders to herd the renegades to the corral, intending to use it as an open cell, easily guarded.

Greg sped off with Moyers and the remainder of the posse. He grimly wondered if the showdown would come at Bar Y. One thing certain, Bart Yates had to be found and made to talk. Only he knew the schemer behind the trouble.

XX

The grim cavalcade came out of the hills and looked down on the dark Bar Y buildings. The riders bunched and Moyers said, "Looks peaceful down there. We might have guessed wrong."

Greg objected. "Yates will have been paid, like Stern, only a lot more. He wouldn't take his cache with him on the raid. Now that the whole thing is blowing up, he'd slip in and out without any fuss, if Edwards knows nothing. If we don't get down there, he'll be gone yonderly for good."

Moyers agreed. "Head for the bunkhouse and be ready for gunplay."

Greg saw Amanda's dark, slim shape on a horse just behind him. He moved his horse to force her to drop back out of the line of fire. The dozen men, fanning out, drifted down the slope and soon the ranch buildings loomed up, as they came in from the rear.

Greg saw the tangle of pens and corrals, the high lift of stable, the long shape of the big ranch house off to his right. He glimpsed the huge tree near the front fence where he had kissed Diana. Then a corner of the dark building cut it off as he moved in beside Moyers to the bunkhouse and cookshack.

The building was dark, with no sign of life. Greg and Moyers could now see the far side of the house. Both men instantly drew rein as they saw a glow of lamplight in two of the windows. Somewhere beyond the house, a horse nickered and one of the posse animals answered, the sound cut off by the rider's clamping fingers. The man cursed softly.

Greg swung out of the saddle and slid the Colt out of his holster. He whispered to Moyers, "Watch the house. I'll give the bunkhouse a look-see."

Amanda said in low urgency, "Sheriff, cover Greg. There's enough of us to watch the house."

Greg cat-footed to the bunkhouse wall and slid along it toward the door, gun held with hammer dogged back. Moyers edged behind him. Greg slanted a look at the house and the glowing windows, glimpsed a moving shadow inside. Bart Yates over there? or waiting with drawn Colt in the darkness of the building at Greg's back?

He took long, silent strides to the door, pressed back against the wall and extended a long arm to the knob, turned it, felt the release. He flung himself onto the door, striking it low with his shoulder. It slammed back as Greg dropped and rolled inside, expecting the blast of a gun.

Silence. He came up against a bunk, caught his balance and stood crouched, ears keening the darkness that eyes could not penetrate. Nothing—empty. Moyers called softly, "Greg?"

"Not here!"

Just then Edwards' hoarse voice challenged from the house. "What's going on out there? Show yourselves or this shotgun—"

"Vale," Moyers sang out. "This is a posse."

The heavy, pain-crooked figure of the rancher appeared

at a corner of the house. Greg jumped to the door and followed Moyers to the old man who waited, shotgun held ready. Greg heard sounds within the house but the lamplight glowed peacefully through the windows. Edwards peered at him and Moyers. Then he saw the dark shadows of the bunched riders beyond.

"What the hell is this?"

"Bart Yates," Moyers snapped. "He's here?"

"With me and Diana. He came in from town and I called him in for a drink." Suddenly he stared at the dark bunkhouse. "But where's the crew? Didn't they sing out at you?"

"Your crew's under arrest. They tried to raid Corwin. Bart led them. There's murder and a whole passel of charges against Yates."

"But—but—my God! He's inside with Diana!"

He swung around but Greg grabbed him. Edwards stumbled and cried out as pain twisted him. Greg grabbed the shotgun from Edwards and shoved it to Moyers then lunged for the house. He heard Moyers shout an order for men to cover the back of the house.

Greg raced up the porch steps, saw the door fully open on the large room he had come to know. He saw grotesque, twisting shadows on the floor within the room and heard Diana's scream. Yates called out, "Step inside and she gets a slug. That goes for any of you!"

Greg froze halfway between steps and door. Men shouted at the rear of the house. Greg stood poised, one foot advanced, Colt lined on the doorway. He balanced the weapon uncertainly. Yates called again. "If anyone's on the porch, step clear. I'm coming out with her."

Greg shot a look at the nearest window. He could see a portion of the room through the curtains, the lamplight mockingly peaceful. The grotesque shadow resolved into the black shapes of two people locked close together. He heard a muffled, tense and tight voice give an order.

192

"Dad! Dad! He has a gun in my back. Let him go to his horse. Please!"

Yates added, "Vale! I mean it. Call off those lawdogs. Have the buggy hitched and brought to the porch."

Vale answered angrily, "Leave her go!"

"Like hell! She's my pass. And jump to that buggy. Give you ten minutes."

"This is the sheriff, Bart. Don't be a fool."

"Don't you be one. Do you want Diana buried because you didn't use your head? What have I got to lose?"

Under the shouting back and forth, Greg had moved to the far end of the porch, circling out to the rail so as not to be framed for Yates' gun. He could now look into the room at an oblique angle. Yates held Diana pressed close against the wall. Greg could see only an occasional tip-swirl of agitated skirt and the toe of a dusty boot.

"The buggy, damn you!" Yates roared.

"Suppose you don't get it?" Moyers defied.

"Then me and Diana come out. Your slugs'll hit her, not me. My horse had better be where I left it, and you'd better stand way back."

"You have to let her go when you mount," Moyers reasoned. "She won't protect you then. So be smart and come out, hands up."

Greg inched toward the house wall as Yates gave a loud, sardonic laugh. "Sure, she won't protect me, so what difference if I gun her where she stands?"

He gave a moment for that to register. "So bring the buggy to the porch. She and me get in, and drive off. You stay where you are and don't trail. I let her go when I know I'm safe. That's the deal. Buggy—or Diana buried."

Silence. Vale cursed, "Damn it, Moyers, bring the buggy."

Moyers answered in reluctant surrender, "You'll get the buggy, Yates."

"Ten minutes," Yates warned.

193

Greg, flattened against the wall, attention on the open, lighted door, wondered what he could do when Yates came out. He'd hold Diana close and he could swing her around as a shield. Greg was in no better position here than any of the men out in the yard.

He bit at his lip as his eyes moved along the porch. He suddenly realized he stood beside a dark window. His mind brought up memory of the interior of the house that he had seen. There was the big main room and then that long hallway leading to the bedrooms. He touched the window sill that must open onto one of them. The hall door would be closed or there'd be a faint glow of lamplight from the main room.

He threw a glance at the open door, holstered his gun and turned to the window. He cautiously touched the frame, hoped against hope and exerted a slow pressure. The lower frame lifted. Unlocked! he breathed in triumph.

Keeping his eyes on the doorway, he slowly worked the window higher. He wished the men in the yard would make noise to cover possible creak of the lifting window. But it moved steadily, slowly and smoothly upward.

He swung a leg over the high sill, groped cautiously within, fearful of a chair or table but his foot encountered nothing. A second later it touched floor and Greg, checking haste for fear of the least sound, worked himself inside.

In the dark room, he palmed Colt from holster to hand. He waited, giving his sight time to adjust to the deeper darkness of the room. He saw the indistinct shape of a bed, a dresser, the gray ovoid of a rug on the floor.

He took a cautious step, froze as Yates' voice came muffled and distorted. "I said just ten minutes. Time's about up!"

"It'll be here," Moyers called reply. "Now don't *you* play the fool!"

Greg moved deeper into the room. Right hand held the Colt and left arm groped into dark nothingness in vain search for the wall. His finger tips touched wood and he brought up sharp. Fingers traced downward—a panel—touched something cold and round—the knob. He wiped moist palm along his levis.

Then he grasped the knob, and pressed knee against the door as he slowly turned, preventing click or scratch of door against frame. He felt the catch release. He became aware of a spiderline of light. It widened bit by bit, to pencil thickness, gun barrel thickness. Six, eight inches; now he saw a portion of the hall, a section of door across the way. He paused, listening. No sound from the big room. He tried to vision where Yates and arm-imprisoned Diana would be standing. Neither could see this door swing inward. He resumed the torturous, opening process, taking a cat's step backward as the door swung wider. He completed the arc and the portal stood completely clear, opposite wall and door in plain view.

He heard a lift of voices outside and a rattle of wheels. Vale Edwards called hoarsely, "We've brought the buggy. If you so much as bruise her wrist, I'll hunt you down and kill you!"

"Just keep those lawdogs calm," Yates answered. "That's all you have to worry about."

Greg knew Yates' attention would be on the porch and yard, ears tuned for the sounds of the buggy. Greg eased inch by inch into the hall, literally trying to flow around the door frame and plaster himself against the wall. The lamplight now fell full on him but he could not see Yates and his captive, meaning that Yates could not see him.

Greg inched along, shoulders pressed flat against the wall. More sounds outside. Then a silence that froze Greg but a few feet from the main room. He heard a man call something, and answer and then Vale's voice lifted. "All right, Bart. It's here."

"Get this!" came Yates' shouted response. "We get in the

195

buggy. My gun will be on her. We stop at the gate and she picks up the reins of my horse. We drive on. If you have any idea about stopping me, Diana gets it then and there. Understood?"

"Understood."

"Then stand back from the porch . . . All right, Diana. We walk out slow. You can get yourself killed with a wrong move."

Greg eased along the wall, faster now, to the corner. He silently stepped out from the wall. Just within the porch doorway, Yates held Diana before him, forcing her arm up behind her back, his Colt muzzle in her side. Both Yates and the girl, held their full strained attention on the porch and what might lurk out there.

Yates called, "Get away from the buggy. That horse will stand. Move, damn you!"

Greg stepped on the thick rug in the main room. It muffled the swift tiptoe of his step. Yates forced Diana into the doorway. Greg quickly came up behind them, lifting his Colt high.

Yates sensed something in the last split second. He jerked half around. The gun muzzle in Diana's side swung away in an instinctive move to meet a new danger. Greg's fingers wrapped around Yates' gun wrist as his own Colt muzzle slammed down on Yates' head. He had twisted Yates' gun wrist down and out. Reflex action from the blow tightened Yates' trigger finger even as he started to fall. The gun exploded with a roar and the slug tore into the doorsill, gouged a long hole along the porch.

Greg pushed Diana out through the door and she stumbled across the porch with the force of the shove. Greg swung around, Colt lining and leveling. Yates hit the floor with a heavy thud. His Colt skittered across the rug to rest under a nearby chair.

Greg heard a yell outside, then Diana's scream and the

rat-a-tat of her heels as she fled down the steps, continuing to scream. Moyers yelled about the hubbub, "Yates!"

Greg called. "It's me—Corwin. Yates is down. Come on in."

He moved aside, keeping his gun on the limp body of the foreman. He saw a twisting rill of blood work through Yates' thick dark hair and wondered if he had killed him. Steps thundered on the porch. Moyers lunged in. Behind him came Amanda, and then the others hurried across the porch.

Moyers came to a rocking halt, seeing Greg and then Yates lying crumpled, one leg drawn up. He bent to the man as Amanda rushed blindly at Greg, threw her arms around him. "You're all right? He didn't shoot—?"

"I'm all right," Greg said, voice muffled in her dark hair.

She broke away, cheeks aflame but her eyes concernedly checked him for sign of injury. The posse pushed through the doorway. Moyers looked up. "I think he'll be all right. You might've cracked his skull, though."

Vale Edwards and Diana, supporting each other, pushed through the crowd. Diana, red hair disheveled and face pale, looked horrified at the unconscious foreman. Then she wonderingly looked to Greg. Her lips tried to form words but she gave a hysterical sob. A second later Greg found another woman clinging to him, crying and shaking.

"It's over. All over. You're all right."

He gently pushed her toward Vale. Amanda watched, color angry and eyes snapping. She whipped away when she met Greg's eyes. Moyers stood up. "We'll get him to Doc Robbins and the jail. He's my prisoner."

Vale demanded, "Will somebody tell me what's going on? Have you all lost your heads!"

Moyers signalled three of the possemen. "Tie him up and put him in the buggy. Greg, we'd better tell Vale before we ride out."

Vale dropped into a chair after Yates had been picked up and carried out. Only Amanda remained standing at the door. Diana fell onto a sofa and sat wide-eyed, still shaking.

Moyers said, "We'll tell you what we know up to now. But there's more coming. We have to get to Redman before word of this gets out."

He outlined the story, most of it familiar, but now revealed in a different and deadly light. Diana and Edwards listened in strickened silence until Moyers finished. Diana spoke in horror. "Why, he wanted to marry me! Wouldn't let any other man so much as look or speak to me. That's why—"

"We had our fight," Greg finished as she turned to him.

Vale said, "I can't believe Bart Yates used me and my ranch to grab off the whole valley!"

Greg glanced warningly at Moyers. "In a way, but someone else had the idea. Yates did the riding, raiding, and killing with a renegade crew he and the other man hired."

"Who?"

"That's why we have to get to Redman and why Yates has to talk before the real devil gets wind of what's going on. If he does, he'll be out of the county as fast as a horse can take him."

He looked at Diana on the sofa, still shaken, and then sharply turned away. Amanda, at the door, searched his face as he and Moyers swept by her. She stood a moment, studying Diana, and then also wheeled and walked swiftly after the men.

198

XXI

Along the dark road to Redman, just after Moyers sent a
rider to order Hoskins to bring his prisoners in immediately,
Bart Yates stirred, groaned and tried to sit up. One of the
men called the sheriff and he and Greg turned back to the
buggy. Moyers swung out of saddle and struck a match, revealing Yates' groggy face. The foreman dully attempted to
move arms and legs, then realized they were bound. His
head came up and his dark eyes flashed the old arrogance
until he saw the sheriff, and Greg at his side.

Moyers said, "Your string played out, Bart. Your road
ends on a gallows, if I know a jury and judge."

"I killed nobody! You know it!"

"You ordered it—and you crippled Wes Zane. Your crew
will tell all they know to keep the rope off their necks. We've
ended a dirty stretch of time in Sioux Valley. You're the
man who came up with the idea. Don't know why yet, but
we'll find out."

Yates glared. His eyes wavered, steadied, wavered again.
"I didn't have any ideas or plan nothing."

"Won't do, Bart. You're it—unless you know more'n we

199

do. But you figure your own chances while we get you to jail."

He turned away. Yates called, "You can't prove anything."

Moyers turned back. "We can. All trails turn right to you. Your crew has dumped you already. They figure an accessory, not really knowing what it was all about, gets less than a hangnoose. So, they've told who gave the orders."

This time he walked on, though Yates cursed after him. Greg followed. Moyers said, "Let him chew on the idea. It might loosen his tongue."

He swung into saddle. The dark miles passed. Amanda looked nervously back at the buggy and Greg had to check his own impulse. He knew who hid behind Yates. Yates could help—cutting out a long period of questioning of the man they planned to trap.

They made the last turn in the road. Ahead, the few lights of Redman looked like little stars. A rider came up from behind, said to Moyers, "Yates wants you."

Moyers instantly called a halt and returned to the buggy. Again Greg stood beside him as Moyers asked, "What now, Bart?"

The foreman looked angry, trapped and frightened. He squirmed against the bonds, subsided and sighed, "If I'm just an accessory and only carried out orders like those I passed on, then what?"

"Jail for a long time. No use telling you different. But the other way . . ."

Yates' mouth twitched. Greg spoke up, "If you don't talk, your friend gets away and you hang. Why, he might even keep on living high in town as he always has."

Yates cursed. "You ruined the whole thing, coming in here just when Hobe Terrall—"

"We're not augering maybes, Bart," Moyers cut in. "You say something or we ride on."

Yates looked defeated, then angry-stubborn, not directed

at those clustered around the buggy. "Fred Unger's your man. He come to me with this scheme. He saw to it I could pay hardcases to come in."

Only Amanda and the other men looked shocked. Greg and Moyers nodded, and Greg said quietly, "Unger planned to get the whole Valley. He made me a force-price when he thought I was getting scared of guns. That was part of the scheme, too, wasn't it?"

Yates hesitated and then growled. "He figured to buy each spread up cheap as we drove you out—one at a time or altogether if you had jumped us."

His eyes spat at Amanda. "You damn near did exactly as we hoped, too. Hal Stern nearly pushed you into our guns."

"Vale Edwards knew nothing?" Greg asked.

"He's a doddering old fool. Oh, Unger figured Bar Y was to catch all the blame until the string played out and we could take it over, too."

"How? You're just the foreman—a hired hand."

"Marry Diana, the flirting, flighty little minx. She kept looking here and there—like at you, Corwin. You weren't the first I drove off. Not in street brawls, though."

Moyers leaned against the buggy. "Suppose it had happened, then what?"

"It was all figured out," Yates said with a flare of twisted, thwarted pride. "Edwards would've had an accident. I'd head Bar Y and Unger'd have all the rest. He'd sell high what he bought cheap."

"Cut the profit with you?"

"I'd have Bar Y. No cut'd equal that."

"There'd be Diana."

"Wife's property is always handled by her husband. Vale gone, I'd have no trouble. Unger figured if there was some kind of will Vale made so Diana had it all, we'd take care of that. I'd be her only heir."

Greg said with mocking wonder, "He had it all figured out, didn't he?"

"Between us we'd—"

"Between us!" Greg demanded, "You fool! If Unger had it planned so close, do you think he'd let the biggest parcel of all slip away from him? Do you figure you'd live any longer'n Edwards when Unger was ready?"

Yates started to protest but his mouth hung open, lips twisted as Greg's logic sunk in. He paled, then shook with anger. "Why that—"

Amanda hurried away to avoid his scorching, blasphemous curses. In the midst of it, Moyers looked at Greg. "We got enough. Why drag it out?"

"Let's get it over," Greg agreed and they turned to their horses.

As they rolled into Redman, Greg leaned toward Moyers and jerked a thumb back toward the buggy. "He's so mad he ain't thinking, and he hates Unger. Why not let 'em meet before we go to the jail? Saves two trips if it works."

Moyers turned off the main street at the next corner. All the houses stood dark and asleep. The sheriff made another turn and then lifted his hand as a signal to stop. Greg saw a big, silent house sitting well back from the street.

The sheriff swung out of saddle, stepped to the buggy and pulled Yates about so he could untie his hands and his feet. He said quietly, "You'll see your trusted friend in a few minutes."

Yates rubbed wrists and ankles then stiffly climbed down from the buggy. He swayed uncertainly and then, between Greg and Moyers, half stumbled up the uneven stone walk to the house. As they mounted the porch steps, Greg saw an increasing glow of light from behind the window in the door.

"Unger's heard us. If he knew what's happened, he wouldn't even—"

They heard bolt and lock click and the door swung open. Moyers quickly moved forward, his big body hiding Yates. Unger, holding the lamp high, peered out.

"Sheriff! What's this all about?" He tried to look beyond the lamp's glow to the street. "I'll swear you've brought a posse. Has something happened?"

Greg moved into the light and Unger looked startled. "Corwin—you, too!"

"Me. A friend of yours paid me a visit, Unger. Happened the sheriff and his posse waited with me to meet him."

"I don't—"

Moyers stepped aside and Yates stood fully in the lamp's bright glow. He glowered angrily and the clotted blood plainly showed in his hair above the ear. Unger's hand, holding the lamp, trembled a second but he assumed a puzzled frown. "Bart Yates? Of course, he's a friend. But I didn't send—"

Yates exploded. "We rode right into a trap. They knew all about it and you're not about to ride off scott free."

Unger eased back and asked in a calm voice, "About what? There's nothing—"

Yates sprang at him but Moyers blocked him. Greg took a stride toward Unger and levelled his Colt on the banker. "Stand hitched."

Moyers restrained Yates with the help of possemen who had come up the walk. Moyers turned to Unger. "We'll spell it out at the jail and later at the trial, Unger. But to say it short, I'm arresting you as accessory to murder—Sam Ralls' —to cattle killing, fence cutting, ambushing Wes Zane and Amanda. By the time court convenes, I'll have a dozen other crimes on the book. We've brought in the Bar Y gunhawks and they've talked. So has Bart here. Now just come along with us peaceful and—"

Unger threw the lamp he held straight at the lawman. Moyers barely warded it off with a spasmodic upward jerk of his arm. The lamp shattered and coal oil sprayed out as the flame snuffed off. Unger swung on his heel and darted toward the door.

Greg's Colt flashed a long stream of orange-red flame toward the banker as it bucked in Greg's fist. Unger's right leg collapsed and, with a scream, he fell just within the doorway. Moyers and Greg jumped toward him at the same moment.

The next two hours passed swiftly. Greg and Amanda rode with Moyers to the jail, a crudely bandaged banker in the buggy and Yates riding double behind a posseman. Doc Robbins came, still rubbing sleep from his eyes, and doctored both Unger and Yates in their cells, then emerged full of questions that Moyers partially answered.

Hoskins and the Bar Y prisoners arrived. They were herded into the jail and Moyers lined them up around the office. Greg indicated the man he knew had ambushed Amanda and he, in turn, implicated two others. Moyers himself indicated two, pitched the cell keys to Greg. "Lock 'em up."

When Greg returned to the office, Moyers glared at the remaining prisoners. "Every one of you has had a hand in this more'n you'll admit. Given time, I'd dig it up and you'd land behind bars. You're lucky I don't have the time."

He paced before them, halted and turned, glaring, then made a curt bob of his head toward the door. "Your horses are out there and be glad of it. If you're seen in this county come sunup—or ever again—you'll rot behind bars. Now get out of my sight and keep going clean beyond the county line."

One cleared his throat. "We ain't got money—"

Moyers grabbed him, spun him back to Greg. "Lock him up. Anyone else want to argue?"

They stampeded out the door. In less than five minutes the last thunder of frantic, racing hoofs faded away. Moyers dropped wearily behind his desk. He looked around at the men who had ridden with him. He smiled at Amanda and then asked Greg, "Do you figure all of us can go home and hang up our guns for good?"

Greg sighed. "Count me for it, anyhow. But it's not wrapped up."

"Just the final sweeping the dirt to the Territorial Prison, friend. Court and judge does that. We're through." Moyers leaned on his desk. "The court'll know what you did to help, Corwin."

"I did nothing but try to keep out of it."

Moyers chuckled, weary and sardonic. "Stubborn about that, ain't you? Thank God, or we could all be gunning and burning down one another! Just what Unger wanted." He dropped back in his chair. "Well, it won't happen. I'll sleep better for knowing it and, the way I feel, I'm ready for bed right now."

He thanked Hoskins and the men who had made up his posse and soon the jail emptied of all but the sheriff and the prisoners. Ranchers and punchers who had ridden for the law mounted horses, many thanking Greg and shaking hands. In a short while only Hoskins, Greg, and Amanda remained.

Hoskins asked, "Riding my way, you two?"

Greg shook his head. "Cal Weber's over in the hotel. I figure to stay in town and ride out with him tomorrow. Lot of work to be done on Tumbling T, now that it's over."

"Amanda?"

She made an embarrassed little gesture. "I—I'll stay in town. It's been a long day."

"Sure has! And a long ride back! See you subsequently."

He mounted and rode slowly away down the street. Greg and Amanda stood alone before the dark courthouse. The minutes passed in a new strain, as though words strove to penetrate an invisible barrier. Finally Greg broke the silence. "Where you staying?"

"At the hotel, if they have a room."

"I'm sure they do."

They walked to the street and Greg picked up the reins of their mounts. "You go ahead and get settled. I'll take care of the horses. See you come morning . . . that is, if you want to ride back with Cal and me."

She nodded and walked away.

When Greg came into the hotel lobby, Amanda sat quite straight and determined in one of the lobby chairs. She jumped to her feet as he approached. He asked, "Don't they have a room?"

"Oh, yes. You'll see when you register."

"You should've—"

"I want to talk to you—outside."

He stared and she flushed, took his arm and led him to the dark porch. Then she dropped his arm as though it burned, walked to the railing and stood looking down the dark street. He came up behind her, puzzled.

She spoke over her shoulder. "Please, just stay there?"

He halted. She traced a finger along the rail a moment, then her shoulders squared. "I like to say what I think. You've heard that. I've made up my mind about you—you and Diana Edwards."

"But she has nothing to do with me."

"I saw that tonight—when we left Bar Y. And there's no one else? here or anywhere?"

He took a step, bringing him directly behind her. "No one."

His hands touched her shoulders and she stiffened, didn't look around. Her words came muffled. "I like it that way. That is, if—"

"No if's, 'Manda."

"Then don't ever let there be . . . anyone else . . ."

"But you? . . . I like it that way, too."

"There could be another war in Sioux Valley—"

His fingers tightened on her shoulders and he swung her around. Lamplight revealed her glowing eyes a moment before he bent to kiss her and his own shadow blended with hers.

Lee E(dwin) Wells was born in Indianapolis, Indiana, the foster son of Robert E. and Nellie Frances Wells. He attended school in Indianapolis and later, in California, studied accounting and became a licensed public accountant and the owner of his own business. With "Pistol Policy" in *Western Aces* (4/41) Wells began publishing Western fiction in the pulp magazine market. As early as "King of Utah" in *The Rio Kid Western* (Winter, 1943), Wells began contributing feature novelettes for Western hero pulps, including feature novelettes for *Range Riders Western*, *The Masked Rider Western* along with more Rio Kid adventures. Authors could take personal credit for these stories as opposed to some hero pulp magazines where writers were forced to work under a house name, such as Wells's Jim Hatfield novelette "Gold for the Dead" in *Texas Rangers* (2/47) as by Jackson Cole. *Tonto Riley* (Rinehart, 1950) was Lee E. Wells first hard cover Western novel. This was followed by such outstanding Rinehart titles as *Spanish Range* (1951) and *Day Of The Outlaw* (1955). The latter was notably filmed as *Day Of The Outlaw* (United Artists, 1959) starring Robert Ryan, Burl Ives, and Tina Louise. Wells learned later in life that his birth name was Richard Poole, and he adopted this as his pseudonym for a number of impressive novels such as *The Peacemaker* (Ballantine, 1954), filmed as *The Peacemaker* (United Artists, 1956), and the outstanding *Danger Valley* (Doubleday, 1968). Whether as Lee E. Wells or Richard Poole, his Western fiction is noted for his wide and vivid assortment of interesting characters and the sense of place and people he could create within his imaginative ranching communities.